KILLER KOALA BEARS
FROM ANOTHER DIMENSION

P. A. DOUGLAS

As water wears away stones, And as torrents wash away the soil of the earth; So You destroy the hope of man.

Job 14:19 New King James Version

Other Severed Press books by P. A. Douglas

The Old One

Epidemic of the Undead

Rancid

Watchers

Hitchers

The Dark Man

Acknowledgements

For this first edition of Killer Koala Bears from another Dimension, my thanks go to everyone at Severed Press, Dane Hatchell, Alan M. Clark, and Sarah VonKain.

Special Thanks (in no particular order)

Thanks to all of you that helped me do that thing that one time. I couldn't have done it without Mina Jones, Sam Slater Boswell, Walker Sherman, Jonathan Realz, Brittany Renee Hagood, David Frost, Alayna Fife, Jimmy Harmon, Eddy Lashney, Shaumi Wilson Todd, Jim Dodge, Barrett Bailey, Aaron Rios, Asa Lane, Nathan Parens, Ben Love, Lauren Marek, Dustin Bryson, and Jay O'Neal. You guys truly are awesome.

1

"I highly doubt this is going to work, Tim." Joana rolled her eyes. She held her shirt out from her waist. It sagged from holding a number of stones.

"I know it is." Tim assured her, removing a stone from her shirt. "Trust me, man, I've done my homework. It's going to work this time. I promise."

"Yeah, right…." She sighed. "Like I haven't heard that before."

"Just watch," he whispered, lifting the stone for her to see. "It's going to open this time. I swear."

Tim grinned, tossing the stone at random across the field. In the stillness of the night, the noise the rock made, as it skittered across the grass seemed much louder.

"Here… hand me another one." He took the stone in his hand. "Only ten more to go." He tossed it at random, this time in a different direction.

Tim Bortimin and Joana Reed had been boyfriend and girlfriend for two years now. If saying that he was the only single guy her age at school wasn't what drew her to him, she'd be lying. She tried to date a few other guys, but nothing ever happened. He was the only boy who really gave her the time of day. Maybe it was because of her weight. She didn't consider herself fat, but in today's world, 198 lbs. at only 4'6" was a little on the chunky side. It also didn't help that they lived in one of the smallest towns ever. West Virginia was like that. It sucked. Bunch of redneck wanna-be's with their deer hunting and sports. Those types of guys didn't even bother giving her a second glance, and in this town that was all she ever got. Her pale, chubby cheeks and black eyeliner was just too much for them. The fact that her long straight hair had streaks of purple in it didn't help the problem either. She was different. Dressed different. Liked a harder version of country music. It was called *Death Metal*. Besides, rednecks didn't understand the complexities of real music. Bands like *Six Feet Deep* and *Napalm Death* just went over their camouflaged, red neck, thick heads. People that didn't understand good music weren't worth her time. She had standards. If it wasn't country, they had no clue. That was another reason why she felt like she ended up with Tim. He was different. Like her, he didn't fit the mold. Sure, not fitting the mold left them both standing out in a large grass field in the middle of the night in the center of town throwing stones. Still, he was growing on her… a little.

"How much longer is this going to take, Tim?" Joana said. "These rocks are getting heavy and I'm tired. We've been out here for over an hour already and you've only thrown six of these damn things."

"You can't rush it, Joana." Tim scoffed, taking another rock and deciding where he wanted to toss it. "That's why this hasn't worked before. We were rushing it. If we really expect to tear a rift and open the portal, then we need to be patient with it. It has to be random. You know this…" He tossed the stone into the field. "We've gone over this already. Just chill."

"You're not the one holding all the damn stones."

Tim rolled his eyes at her.

"But what if old man, Terry Wilson, wakes up? I'm not in the mood to get shot at tonight."

"Oh, come on. That old creep's dead asleep and you know it. Long as we keep quiet he won't even know we're out here. Besides…" He pulled his long jet black hair out off his face and looked toward the old man's house. "We're far enough away. We could make more noise if we wanted. He's not going to hear a thing."

He took another stone from Joana's shirt and tossed it at random into the grass. It collided with something when it hit. The loud noise *pinged.* Both of them stiffened and looked toward the old man's house. The echoing sound faded. After a moment, Tim took another stone.

"See… told you he wouldn't wake—"

"I still don't see how randomly tossing stones in someone's yard is going to open a portal to another world. This all seems a little silly."

"These aren't just any stones, Joana!"

"Shhh… Keep your voice down." She ducked low as if reducing her height would help the darkness conceal her location. "Well, if it does work, which I'm not saying it will, what the hell do you expect to be on the other side?"

"Does it really matter, man?" He scratched his nose ring and leaned forward, kissing her cheek. Reaching into her shirt to take another stone, he said, "Where ever it leads, it's got to be better than this. Aren't you tired of this town? I'm tired of the looks I get from these people just because I chose to be gothic and not some tree hugging redneck. It's like they haven't ever seen someone dress in all black before. I refuse to be one of them. I'm not going to live the rest of my life in a stupid deer stand."

"I never said you had to." Joana hated it when he started ranting like this. He could be so negative.

"I promise… this is going to work this time. I've got it down to a science." Tim lifted the stone to his mouth, breathed hot air on it and rubbed it on his shirt as if to polish it. "I'm telling you, these are going to do the trick. When that rift opens up and we leave this shitty town, you'll thank me."

He tossed the rock into the dark. Joana flinched, watching it sail across the air. She gritted her teeth, waiting for that moment when it would collide with something hard, waking old man Terry Wilson. It didn't. Instead the stone settled into the grass, silent. The tension in her body momentarily released, at least long enough for Tim to throw another rock.

"Hand me another one."

Nearly another thirty minutes seemed to pass while Tim took his time tossing each stone into the field behind Terry's house. Between each toss, Joana listened to him continue to rant on and on about society and the depravity of creative reasoning. The boy sounded smart… until you started actually listening. Realistically he could have just taken all of the stones into one big handful, tossing them all at the same time. Had he done that, they would have been able to make it over to the diner before it closed for the night. Joana would have liked that. Expecting to have been done way earlier, she hadn't eaten anything before the trip to old man Terry's house. She was hungry and it was getting late. Instead, the young high school senior insisted on taking his time. He wanted it to be right. Had she known that, she would have snacked on something before they left her house earlier.

Still, Tim insisted.

If it was going to work, it had to be done right. Joana did her best to hide that she was upset for missing the diner before it closed. It was the only place in town that stayed open until midnight.

But finally, they were done. Fifteen minutes had passed and Tim was still standing there in the middle of the field just waiting. Nothing had happened.

At least Joana was finally done toting those stupid rocks.

"Well… I thought you said this was it. I don't see any *riftsssssss*…" She shoved her fists, one against each wide hip.

"Just give it a minute. It has to work this time. It just has to."

"Come on, Tim. We've been standing here for more than fifteen minutes. Isn't that enough? Can we just go… please? I'm hungry."

"You're always hungry." Tim breathed, clearly taking out his frustration on her.

"What the hell is that supposed to mean?"

"Nothing. Let's just go. Maybe we can hit the diner. They should still be open. You think?"

"Yeah… sure, I bet they're still open." She rolled her eyes and shook her head, turning to walk back toward the car.

As quietly as possible the two crept past the old man's house and down the street. To keep him from hearing them upon arrival they were smart enough to park a few blocks away and walk up. That had been

Joana's idea. Tim swore up and down that the walk was a waste of time. Old man Terry wasn't going to hear them. He was nothing but an old drunk. As they made the walk back, she couldn't help but think about that. Hell, if anything were a waste of time, it was throwing stones in someone's yard for two hours in the middle of the night. Sometimes she had no idea why she put up with Tim. He was cute. They liked the same music. Liked the same style clothes. They were the only two gothic kids in this dump of a town, but that didn't mean she should have to put up with half of his crap. She knew that gothic people were supposed to be into some weird stuff. Anyone could tell you that. Just look at all of those *Marilyn Manson* music videos. But man, half of the activities that Tim could come up with for them to do... he needed to spend less time playing World of Warcraft and spend more time filling out college applications. If he wanted to get out of town that bad, his best bet was through a college grant. Not something make-believe like quantum mechanics. He spent way too much time in his fantasy world. And for that, their relationship was suffering.

Joana could only take so much. How much more, now that was the question. He was on thin ice already.

After reaching the beat-up rust bucket that was Joana's mom's car, they set off toward town. She kept her mouth shut while Tim suggested they stop in at the diner. Looking at the clock, she knew better than that and just headed home instead. She'd just have to settle for something at the house before bed. Of course, she'd have to drop Tim off first.

As they turned down the winding unlit roads, Joana wondered, among other things, when Tim planned to get a car of his own. He was the only 18 year old she knew of in town that didn't have one. For her it seemed like tonight would end no differently than any other night. Disappointment in her boyfriend. Elsewhere, that was beginning to become entirely another story.

Back at old man Terry Wilson's house the darkness began to shift.

Terry Wilson awoke to what he thought was someone shining their headlights into his bedroom window. Only, his bedroom window didn't face the street. It faced the back yard and the seven acres of land that sat beyond.

The light was odd. Hues of deep purples and baby blue fluttered into his room forcing him to sit up. Without second thought the 76 year old war veteran stepped into his boots, grabbed the shotgun from beside the bed, and stepped out of his room to investigate. His massive beer belly protruded out like a bulbous tumor as he made his way through the house wearing nothing but his whitie-tighties and boots. Reaching the kitchen, he started to hear rustling noises near the house. Someone was out there, no doubt about it.

Stupid motherfuckers... Damn kids best not be pickin' them 'shrooms on my property again.

Truth was no kids ever picked anything on his property. He didn't have a single cow to his name.

No manure, no mushrooms. That hadn't stopped the old man from calling the cops half a dozen times in the last year. Swore up and down that the youth in the area were doing drugs on his property. He was just a loopy old man.

Lonely and scared.

Scared of being alone, which he had been for quite some time.

He scratched three weeks' worth of growth on his graying chin just as he reached the back door. Something shambled on the other side, banging against it. Startled, Terry jumped. The abrupt movement actually forced a bit of gas from the old man's rear. And just when he was starting to giggle about it, a purplish-blue light appeared, leaking through the kitchen window. Same as what woke him to begin with.

He gripped the shotgun tight. He cocked it, checking the chamber. Two shells. Hopefully that would be all he needed. With any luck he wouldn't even need those. It had been so long since he had last fired the stupid thing, he wasn't even sure it would fire. He swallowed hard and reached for the door.

"Whoever the hell's out there… you better get of my property right now!" His voice shook. "I got my shotgun and I aims to use it!" he shouted, doing his best to sound confident.

Whatever was on the other side of the door fell silent and Terry thought for a split second that raising his voice was all it was going to take to force the trespassers to be on their way. He felt the tension in his chest slacken, his back slumping low, which forced his belly to bulge out even more.

"Fuck… I'm gettin' too old for this shi—"

Something slammed against the door, hard.

Terry jumped, almost dropping the shotgun.

He heard even more noises. There was more than one of them out there. His heart raced. The light flooding the kitchen through the window illuminated the area in an eerie glow. Blues and purples danced across his refrigerator and tile floor.

He tried to see outside through the window, but the light was too much for his aged eyes.

A long slender object slammed through the window next to the back door. Glass shattered, falling to the floor. The object was there one second and gone the next. It almost looked like a spear of some kind. Terry couldn't tell in the darkness and fluttering colors. It moved too fast. More noises erupted outside, followed by a persistent banging at the door. Whoever was outside wanted in. That was for damn sure. On the other hand, what they were saying wasn't clear. A lot of odd grunts and hisses that didn't seem natural. Didn't sound like noises a man would make.

The spear jutted though the window again, staying long enough for Terry to determine that it was in all actuality, a spear. He took two steps back, bumping into the counter near the sink. His eyes shifted from the window to the door, and then to the window again. He lifted the shotgun at the ready and tried steadying his aim. His arms and hands shook both from nerves and old age.

"I… I said… get of a my property now… befo—"

A hand reached into the window. Terry felt his heart stop. It wasn't like any hand he had ever seen. It was covered in hair and had long pointed fingernails sharp enough to kill a man.

"What the hell is—"

The backdoor to the kitchen kicked open, swinging inward fast. It slammed against the wall and Terry jumped. The gun went off making him flinch again. It jolted his body as the shell exited the barrel. The loud report echoed through the house. His ears rang. A few drops of urine drizzled from his dick soaking the front of his whitie-tighties.

The silhouetted figured at the door fell back into the grass outside. Terry saw it happen. His jaw fell agape as he watched the buckshot spread across the intruder's chest in the darkness. He had never actually shot a trespasser in all his life. Sure, he'd had to give out more than half a dozen verbal threats each year with all the teenagers and hunters crossing his property, but never actually had to do it. His skin suddenly felt hot, then ice cold. His blood pressure rose. Like he had said, he really *was* too old of this shit.

Forgetting about the others he had heard, the sudden noise farther out in the yard startled him back into action. He raised the shotgun. It bobbed up and down as he took several slow steps toward the door. He needed to get a look. Needed to call the cops and probably an ambulance. He gripped the gun tighter, trying to keep it from shaking, but it did no good. As he reached the door, he could see the figure still lying in the grass where it had fallen, the figure's chest full of holes. Taking a quick glance away from the body, he looked out into the yard. In several random spots there were various lights. Some bigger than others. But where was the light coming from? He looked around, puzzled by what he was seeing. Each spot that was lit up seemed to have no natural source. The light was the source, just floating in mid-air like some type of magic trick. He waved the barrel of the shotgun around a few more times, skimming the perimeter. He saw no one, just the bizarre lights. He heard no other strange noises.

Maybe I was just hearin' things and this fella here was the only one. Sure as hell sounded like more than one.

He looked down at the unmoving body before him. In the darkness, and with all of that odd light dancing around in the yard, the figure on the ground was cast in shadows. Terry found that peculiar. That much light should have pushed the shadows away, but instead it seemed to be creating more darkness. He looked around in the yard one more time for good measure, and then reached to his side, flicking the light switch on the wall in the house. The back porch light kicked on, illuminating the body.

Terry Wilson gasped.

"What the hell… is this shit?"

It was like a man, but it wasn't a man at all.

It was a monster. An abomination. It had the body structure of a large man. It was covered in a thick coat of gray fur and had abnormally big ears like that of some bears. Its nose was flat and drawn in close. The creature had long sharp claws. In some respects, it kind of reminded Terry of a raccoon. He'd had countless of those types of trespassers, the likes of which he did have the luxury of shooting at a time or two. But how could this exist? It was the body structure of a man. When he'd shot it, it was standing up-right like a fucking human. Upon closer inspection, he determined that the thing was for sure dead. It wasn't moving or breathing. The countless holes, in and around the creature's chest, leaked red. Terry had pretty much hit the thing dead center. Just to be sure, he reached down, prodding the being on the leg with the barrel of the shotgun.

As he leaned in jabbing its leg, he realized something else.

It was wearing clothes. The clothing was primitive, but it was clothing just the same. The man-animal was wearing a necklace made of bone and had some type of makeshift cloth wrapped around its waist covering what Terry could only assume was its gender-parts.

He was so elated with the odd and unexpected creature and the lights still flickering in the yard that he felt like it was all a dream. Any minute now, he would wake up in his king size bed fit for two all alone, ready to face a new day. Alone. He was too busy staring at the thing lying in the grass before him, contemplating this crazy dream he found himself in. Too busy in fact, he didn't hear the window in the living room break. Or the intruder climbing into the house. He didn't hear the footsteps drawing closer, creeping up behind him. His eyes were wide, his mind flustered with questions. Namely, where the hell this thing came from… It could be big boot, maybe… and what where those lights in the—"

When Terry Wilson heard the thing step up behind him in the kitchen and felt it breathing down the back of his neck, it was too late. He didn't even have time to spin around. He felt a sudden sharp pain in his back, and in that same instant, just like the kitchen window, a long slender spear punctured his chest. Only this time it wasn't glass that shattered to the floor. The creature jabbed it further and Terry watched it extend farther out before him. Meat and blood covered sinew clung to the sharp tip of the spear. Terry couldn't breathe. He looked down at his chest and realized then that the chunks of meat and muck on the end of the sharp object were his own internal bits. He coughed, trying to gasp for air. Crimson spewed from his lips as his mouth filled with the iron taste of warm blood. He gagged swallowing most of it down. His left arm fell limp to one side, dropping the shotgun. It *clinked*, coming to a rest in the grass. His other hand grabbed at the rod sticking out of his sternum. His hand slipped on the wooden pole and came away red. His vision wavered and his knees buckled. For a second or two he even felt as if he were floating in midair. It was then that he realized that the creature holding the spear was holding him up. His legs and arms were just dangling, limp and lifeless. The creature must have let go, because Terry then fell to his knees. Everything started to go black. He thought of his ex-wife and how he missed her. Remembered what it had been like all those years ago to share that big bed. It had been lonely without her. Just as he started trying to remember her face, something out in the yard distracted him.

Something was coming out of the floating lights.

More monsters.

Terry Wilson fell forward, the spear still shoved through his midsection. He was dead before his corpse even hit the grass next to the creature he had just killed.

2

Lewisburg was a charming little town and that's how the towns-people liked it. Great coffee. Food enriched with character. Shop owners dedicated to the customer. And yes, the Victorian look that couldn't be found in any other place. Houses in the town were classic Victorian-era two and three story variety, and quaint one story cottages. Of course, like any other small town, it had its share of dilapidated mobile homes. The grass was kept trim and tight in the areas where it grew, which wasn't much of anywhere. Most of the land was dry sands and thick clay. A small town like Lewisburg is usually lucky if there's a decent one-screen movie theater, maybe a community dance troupe. But a bowling alley? This speck on the map in the Greenbrier River Valley laid claim to one of the first bowling leagues in the country. But a claim to the past is about all it held. The lanes were long torn out and thrown away. Erected in 1902, the building now served as Lewisburg's creative control tower, attracting an unlikely band of artistic characters, back-to-the-land types, and retirees.

The large mountains that nestled around the valley and the river, in truth, were what kept the economy going. With only one way in and out of town on Highway 105, it was easy to show up and never leave. That's how most locals got to be locals. Visited and decided there was no reason to go. It was a perfect slice of heaven. The tourist attraction of mountain climbing, hiking, and whitewater rafting was a staple to the small community. Without the spring and summer seasons of great outdoors, things would have definitely been different.

Right after dusk, before the night took hold, things always quieted down. Aside from occasionally hearing Frank Edelman's four-wheeler wreaking havoc through the many trails surrounding the town on the weekends, all that could be heard was the wildlife. Owls hooting on their perch. Wild dogs howling in the night, communicating with one another from long distances. Crickets and frogs got so loud at night that, at times, they would drown out Frank and his four-wheeler in the woods.

A lot of the townsfolk would argue the town was dying. With the sudden economic recession and the election in full tilt, many would say that Obamacare was to blame for all of the problems. That wasn't the case. Every business had its slow seasons and Lewisburg, West Virginia was run like a small business. Things would pick up. They always did.

Some would even venture to say 3,830 is a pretty large number. Well, it would be if we were talking about the number of light bulbs Frank Edelman changed at the bowling alley-turned Recreation Center every month. But that wasn't what they're talking about. That was the town's population. Sure, there are a lot smaller towns in America, mind you. However, compared to the census taken back in 1902, that number had surprisingly dropped rather than increase. Although a lot of visitors would drop in and never leave, this was more of a retirement town. The death rate just never did seem to even out with the new arrivals. You would guess that was to be expected. It was in the middle of nowhere.

Frank had worked at the old Recreation facility almost his entire life. Well, his adult working life that is. With his 22nd birthday only a few months away he had already put in more than five years as the janitor. No matter how often he tried to argue that he was the custodial staff, his friends would just remind him what that meant: Janitor. So what if he cleaned the bathrooms, mopped the floors, serviced the AC until nearly as old as the building, and changed the light bulbs? Someone had to do it. He enjoyed the job and made good money, too. At least that was what he told himself on nights like tonight. Tomorrow was to be some big local art opening for some of the retired folks. They already had the inside transformed into a gallery of sorts. It was his job to make sure everything else was in working order before the big opening the next day. Check all the lights, change any that were blown, clean the bathrooms extra well, mop *and wax* the halls, and take out the trash.

He hated it when they had big events like this coming up. Especially on such short notice. He was finally down to the last item on the list, which was taking out the trash.

The back door to the Center swung open. Frank strolled out with a full bag of trash slung over each shoulder. The MP3 player in his back pocket was on shuffle. *Wish You Were Here* by Pink Floyd blared through the ear-buds. Although small, the headphones could crank out some noise. He had to walk about twenty paces before reaching the dumpster at the back of the building. Once there, he dropped both heavy loads of trash at his feet. His head bobbed in rhythm with the music. The night sky was clear and the moon high overhead. The moon was bright tonight. The mountains that wrapped around the Lewisburg valley were illuminated in its wondrous glow.

Unlike a lot of friends his age, Frank loved it out here. It was quiet and a lot of times, breathtaking.

He stretched his back and pulled out a pack of smokes from the front pocket of his blue coveralls. He wore the bulky jump-suit looking outfit when he worked to keep his actual clothing clean. The building was so old and dusty that every night after work his coveralls were generally in bad shape.

The song by Pink Floyd ended, giving way to *Jesus Freak* by DC Talk. He laughed out loud at the memories that the song brought to the surface. He hadn't listened to it in ages. With enough songs on his device to last a decade, he hardly ever heard the same song twice in a given month. He lit up a cigarette and stuffed the pack of Lucky Strike's back in his front pocket.

A plume of smoke fluttered from his lips. He lifted the sleeve of his coveralls checking the time.

"Fuck, man…" He cursed at the time, aggravated that he hadn't finished all of this up hours ago. "Kathie is going to have a cow."

At least he was off tomorrow and currently getting paid time and a half. If he had it his way, he would spend most of the afternoon running around on his four-wheeler.

He smiled at that and stood there by the dumpster enjoying his little smoke break. It felt good to finally be done. Dump the trash, lock up, and then he could go home.

With the last drag of the cigarette pulling deep into his lung, he held it in to savor the taste. He dropped the butt to the cement and looked down, stomping it with one steel-toed boot. Just as he was about to reach over and heave one of the hefty bags of trash into the dumpster something caught his attention from the corner of his eye. Something blue flickered a few feet away in the darkness. When he looked up it was gone. He pulled the left bud from his ear and looked out past the dumpster for a moment.

"Ehh… your mind playing tricks on you again, man. These long nights are getting to you." He shook his head putting the ear-bud back in place, reached down, and tossed a bag of trash into the dumpster.

As the bag crashed in notes of breaking glass, it echoed across the stillness and silence.

Suddenly spooked, Frank took one more hard look out beyond what his eyes could see. He shook his head and reached down for the second bag.

There it was again… only larger. Blue and purple. The light pulsated in the distance in midair for a second and then was gone. Just when he was about to pass it off as an acid trip flashback, the fluttering light returned and stayed. He watched as it grew with each pulsing throb. Like a vertical eye, it just grew and grew, lighting up the area around it.

"What the fuck is that…" He stood curious with his brow raised.

Oh yeah, he was definitely having an acid flashback. No question about it. Been a long time since one of these happened. He hadn't been one to do a lot of drugs when he was younger, but that LSD, it stayed with you. Last time he saw hallucinations was when he accidentally cracked his back trying to lift a heavy box at his mom's house. This was no different. He must have just lifted that garbage bag wrong or something. Pulled a muscle. As he watched the strobing light reach its max size his eyes grew wide. Someone or something was climbing through the light. Like it was some type of portal or something.

He chuckled, straightening his spine while pressing one hand against the lower back. Funny thing was he didn't feel like he pulled anything. He felt fine. Even so, he watched in awe as the bear-like man stepped out of the light. Then another, and another. Each stepped out and surveyed the area.

Haaa... Franked laughed to himself. *Looks like a fucking koala bear or some shit.*

He shrugged, still owing the occurrence to his old days of drug use. "I ain't got time for this crap." He reached out, grabbed the last bag of trash and tossed it into the dumpster.

The sound of the heavy bag reverberated off the metal walls of the dumpster. What happened next, Frank would have never thought possible.

"Ereht revo!" One of the creatures shouted, pointing its long sharp spear at Frank.

Frank swallowed hard and gasped, expecting the visual relapse to have gone away by now. He stood frozen in shock and wonder as three of the bear-men started to approach. More stepped out through the blue and purple beam of light.

"Kcatta!" One of them shouted.

Instantly, the three approaching figures started to charge. Frank stepped back and almost stumbled.

"Hey… I don't mean to—"

His words were cut short by a sharp pain in his right shoulder. His gaze followed the sensation and he promptly recognized the source of the pain. A short slender wooden spear was protruding from his right shoulder nearly three inches. He grabbed at it and almost felt to his knees from the pain. A deep red ran down the sleeve of his coveralls. The blue fabric had torn and his shoulder felt warm and wet on top of the pain.

Frank screamed, stumbling and struggling to stand.

His attackers' pace quickened.

Frank's mind blurred. The koala-looking motherfuckers were only a few paces away when he felt his legs work against his mind. He didn't realize it yet, but with the spear still lodged in deep, Frank was running toward the back door. His right arm wasn't moving. As his body forced him forward, it slumped limp at his side. His mind caught up with his legs when his vision returned and he was pulling the door open and falling into the Rec Center.

Throbbing pain bore down on him as he collided with the floor, the small wooden thing sticking out of his shoulder slamming against the floor where he fell. He heard something snap and for a split second was pretty sure it was his arm.

With the adrenaline flowing, he pushed the sudden unbearable sound out of his mind and spun around on his ass. He slammed the door shut with his feet and pressed them against the door, still struggling to catch his breath. The door immediately jolted. The aggressors wanted inside. Pounding fists ensued. The door shook.

"Fuck…" Frank barked, still seated on the freshly waxed floor. When he spun around on his ass he felt the MP3 player in his back pocket crack. The music resonating from his earphones was no more. With that, the pounding fists seemed even louder. "What the hell is going on?"

He gasped, finding the energy to stand.

Digging past his cigarettes with his left hand he pulled the keys from his right pocket and locked the door.

His heart raced and his breathing grew heavy. His arm throbbed. He couldn't bring himself to look at it. He needed to keep those things from getting in. He looked around for anything to use as a weapon or to just barricade the door for more support. There was nothing.

And just when the thought of '*nothing*' danced around in his head, the pounding outside ended. The door became still.

He stood there for a while, his one good hand shaking. It wasn't until he looked down at his right shoulder that he realized what had happened was real. It had actually happened. The sound that he thought had been his arm snapping like a twig when he fell was in fact the end of the wooden spear. The handle was snapped to one side, still clinging by just a few loose slivers of wood.

"Ahh… shit." Pain surged though his limp arm as he grabbed the spear with his left. "What the hell is going on?" He winced, forcing himself to try using his right hand. The pain was excruciating. The hand flexed and his elbow budged just a little, but not much.

He listened to the silence for a minute, but heard nothing outside. Nothing close to the door at least.

"How the hell am I supposed to get this out of my shoulder? Fuck, that's going to hurt." Frank didn't want to think about pulling the spear free. There was no telling how deep it was.

Favoring his left hand, he used it to lean against the wall and started easing himself down the hall toward the front of the Center. With each step, the broken spear handle bounced up and down, reminding him each time how much it hurt.

He needed to get to the doctor and get his shoulder looked at. Make sure his arm was going to be okay. His car was parked in the front and that was where he was headed.

Still trying to wrap his mind around what had just happened, he reached the front double sliding-glass doors. In the glass he saw his reflection, the small broken spear dangling there just like his useless arm. The sleeve of his coveralls was soaked a dark crimson. At night the sensors were off because he had everything locked down. He reached in his pocket again. Awkwardly with his left hand he started fishing for the key in his right pocket and heard something out in the parking lot. He looked out. His white 1982 GMC Jimmy wasn't even forty feet away. He could make it.

Then he saw it. Out past his car. Another ominous light started to form in the parking lot. Same as before. It pulsed and grew. Before he even put the key in the front door, figures started to climb out stepping into the street.

"Fuck this." Frank spat.

He zipped down his coveralls, reaching deep down to his actual jean pockets. Retrieving his cellphone, he called 911. With just the one hand, the task was hard, but he pulled the phone out just the same.

The phone rang.

"Thanks for calling. Please state your emergency." The operator said calmly.

"I need the police right away."

"Hold please…"

Before Frank had a chance to say another word, the phone began ringing again. It rang several times before anyone picked up. He watched out in the street as the bipedal animals began to spread out, scanning the area. It was as if they were looking for something. Then he saw several of them point in a direction and start running that way. Frank tried to see but couldn't get a good look from his vantage point. What followed told all he needed to know. The sound of someone screaming boomed across the parking lot, reaching his ears, even past the thick glass of the sliding doors. For a second he thought no one was going to answer the phone.

"Lewisburg Police department." The woman said, very mater-of-fact.

"I need help! Something is fucking going down! We need all of the cops hitting the—"

"Calm down… Who is this—Where are you?"

"Frank Edelman. I work down at the Rec Center. Listen to me…" Frank started, panic setting in. "We need to get some cops down here right away. Bring guns. Lots of fucking guns!"

"What is happening exactly, Mr. Edelman?" The lady on the other end was so relaxed that it was as if Frank was calling about an issue with the router from his internet provider.

"Are you hearing a word I'm saying?"

"Yes, but I need you to tell me what's happened."

"You wouldn't believe me it I told you."

"Well, I'm not just going to send someone down for nothing. I need you to—"

"Hell, you're going to need to send more than just someone. Send them all! I've got a fucking spear in my arm for crying out loud. A bunch of…" Frank paused, knowing the truth would sound silly. "A bunch of looters are loose over here. They tried to break into the Rec Center. Attacked the shit out of me!"

The operator said a few things, but in truth, Frank wasn't listening. His attention had been drawn back to the parking lot and beyond.

The call ended. From what he made of it someone was on their way, which was good.

Frank watched from the safety of the locked glass doors with absolute horror. What he was witnessing couldn't be real. Whoever they had chased down in the street was now in view. He watched as three of the bear-like figures dragged the man by the legs across the gravel kicking and screaming. His attackers didn't seem to notice. A fourth creature walked up with a spear in hand. Frank felt his heart pounding against his ribcage as he watched. He had an idea of what was coming.

A deathblow to the chest perhaps.

What happened was much worse. The moonlight illuminated everything in gruesome detail.

With one swift strike, the fourth creature lunged with the spear jabbing at the man's stomach. Blood spurted into the air. The man howled in agony. All four of the hairy figures raised their arms with excitement. If hovering over the poor helpless man and watching him bleed out wasn't enough, the creature jabbed him again. With the clear strike, something dark and shiny spilled out across the pavement. The figure with the weapon stepped away. And that was when it started. The other three monsters started to feast. Ravenous and malicious, they used their sharp claws to yank and pull at the bits of shiny substance. As it reached their lips, it coated their furry faces in that same shiny moonlit glow. Frank realized what it was. The man's intestines had been strewn out across the parking lot and these freaks of nature were eating him from the inside out.

Frank gagged and felt bile rise in his throat. He forced it back and took another look. The point that he couldn't hold the vomit back any longer was when he realized the dying man wasn't dead. He was still alive while they feasted on his exposed guts and gore.

Frank puked.

The warm smell of cheesy nachos splashed across the freshly waxed floor at his feet. When he was done, he wiped his mouth and looked out to the street again.

The creatures were gone. The man was alone, unmoving.

Dead.

Franks phone rang in his left hand and it made him yelp. Forcing his good arm over his mouth, he looked outside and stood still. The phone rang a few more times while he investigated.

Sure that he hadn't given away his location with that God-awful shout, he looked down to see who was calling him. Kathie, his girlfriend's photo popped up on the screen with her number below it. His fears seemed to lift just by the thought of her.

"Hey baby," he said, answering the phone.

"Oh my God, please help me! They're gonna get me! They already ate Captain! Oh my Go—"

"Honey! Kathie… Baby! Hello!"

The call ended.

He dialed her back right then. The phone rang once and went straight to voice mail. He hung up and called again.

It rang twice. "Come on, baby… pick up… fuck… fuck…"

The answering machine again.

"Kathie, I'm on my way home! Get somewhere safe!" He paused. "I'm coming… Baby… I love you."

Kathie was in trouble and their three year old Wirehaired terrier was dead.

This just couldn't be happening.

Frank felt faint and his shoulder throbbed.

3

"Hey…" Tim pointed. "You just passed the street we need to take to get to the diner. What gives?"

"What… *gives*, Tim. Really?" Joana's grip tightened on the steering wheel. Forcing out a smile across her chubby cheeks, she said, "Do you even realize what time it is? We spent nearly two hours out at that old creep's house. The diner's closed. I'm taking you home and then I'm going to bed."

The car moved slowly down the rural streets of downtown. All of the shops were closed, most all of the sale signs turned off. Other than a few parked cars in front of some of the small businesses, the narrow street seemed like a ghost town. It always gave Joana the jitters when she drove around the small town at night alone. Riding around with Tim was basically the equivalent of driving alone. If they were ever to be put in a dangerous situation, she would be the one defending him rather than the other way around. He was as worthless as one could get.

The car rolled to a stop at the four-way. Although they were the only car on the street, out of habit, Joana looked both ways and then started down the road again. One of Korn's new songs quietly played through the speakers. She wasn't one for turning the music up ungodly loud like Tim.

"But you can't drop me off at my house," Tim insisted, rolling down the window.

The cool air felt nice, so Joana did the same. "And why the hell not?"

"Because the 'rents think I'm staying at Pete's… remember?" Tim's eyes went wide as if she were supposed to have remembered something she had yet to have been told.

"So, am I taking you to his house then?"

"Well… I was kind of thinking that—"

"No. You can forget that." Joana shook her head, cutting Tim short. "I'm gonna get in trouble as it is if my parents catch me trying to sneak back into the house this late. You know how they are about that crap!"

"Hey… don't raise your voice at me just because your parents are the strict ones."

"Look who's talking," Joana argued, not taking her eyes off the road. Doing a U-turn toward Pete's house, she barked, "I'm not the one telling lies about where I'm staying."

Tim looked like he was about to refute the statement. Instead, he pulled some of his long black hair from his face and turned his attention to things passing by outside of the car.

"What? You don't have anything to say to that one, do you?"

"Hmmm…" Tim snorted, as if thinking something he knew he better not say.

"What… Don't act like you aren't thinking it…" Joana stopped the car at the same four-way once more, this time going the opposite direction toward Pete's house.

The car idled. The only sound in the street was that of the humming motor.

She waited, her head cocked to one side, eyes locked on Tim.

Tim just shook his head. Joana put the car in park and crossed her arms. The mix on her CD changed from the new song by Korn to one of her all-time favorites: Acid Bath's *Scream of the Butterfly*.

"Fuck…" Tim slung his arms up as if in defeat. "What the hell am I supposed to do with you, huh? All you ever do is bitch."

"Where the hell is that coming from?"

"The stones are heavy, this… it's late that…" Tim said, his voice a mocking nasally pitch. "I'm hungry, this… You lie to your parents, that… Shit, girl… if you ain't running that damn trap at me its only because your busy stuffing it."

"Excuse me?" She winced, trying like hell to keep the tears from flooding.

Joana's bottom lip quivered.

"Oh, now you gonna start tearing up on me, too?"

"What the hell is your problem, Tim?" Joana began to cry. "I didn't do anything. I don't deserve to be treated like this." Her thick eyeliner and mascara started to run down her rounded cheeks. She wiped at it with one hand, only smearing it more. "I don't know why I put up with you, you know that? There are plenty of guys out there that would treat me a whole hell of a lot better than your sorry ass. Grown men… that… that don't throw stupid stones in the middle of the night because… because of some fantasy game!" She breathed deep, finding her voice among the sobs. "You need to grow up, get a job, get a car… and get a life!"

There, she finally said it. It had been eating away at her for months now and finally it was out. As those closing words danced across her lips into the air, she felt lifted. Lighter. She had needed to, wanted to, say that for a long time. It was out. How she really felt was on the table. She took a deep breath and paused, hoping that what she had just said was sinking into her boyfriend's thick skull.

What Tim did next was unexpected.

He began to laugh.

The sound felt like a sharp jab to Joana's gut. He couldn't be serious.

"You? Get better guys than... or sorry... '*men*', than me?" He used quotation fingers. "Give me a break. You and me are the only two people in this stupid town with the same interests. And besides... let's face it. You're fat."

"Ohhh!" Joana huffed, balling a fist in the air. Her chubby cheeks seemed to boil, her eyebrows squishing into her face. "That's it! It's over. Get out! Just get out! You can walk to Pete's, or where ever the hell it is you plan on staying tonight."

"Awe, come on." Tim's demeanor became soothing. "Pete's house is like a twenty minute walk from here. Besides, he is probably already asleep."

"Well, you should a thought about that before becoming such an asshole." Joana locked stares with him and then glared at the passenger side door.

Tim got the hint and reached for the handle. "Look, Joana. I'm sorry. You know how I feel about—"

Tim stopped in mid-sentence, his attention drawn to the middle of the street less than a block up ahead.

"What the hell is that?" Joana saw it, too.

"What are they doing?" Tim asked, the argument seemingly forgotten.

"I don't know." She whispered with a sniffle.

Up the street ahead two lone figures wearing strange clothing dragged something into the street. Whatever it was, it was a good size.

"Are they wearing Mickey Mouse Club hats?"

"I don't know. It's hard to see."

Even with her headlights on, the events unfolding before them were cast in shadows. Whatever it was they were doing, it was odd. Wrong. With their windows down, even from that far up, they could hear the scraping sounds as the two figures pulled the large object across the pavement. Tim and Joana didn't speak. They just looked on, dumbfounded.

The two creepy figures stopped in the middle of the street and leaned over whatever it was they were carrying. They were doing something to it. A faint yelp from that direction eased its way into the car. Joana heard it clear as day over the hum of her idling car.

"That sounded like a dog. What the hell are they doing to that poor thing?" She said, leaning into the steering wheel as if that would help get a better look.

"I don't think that's a dog. Honk the horn at them. Maybe that'll scare'em off."

Just as Joana was about to protest the idea, Tim reached between her chest and arms, pressing the horn for her. He hit it with three quick taps. The horn sounded ominous as it blared across the darkness in the unlit street.

"What the hell did you do that…" Joana gasped. "Oh, God."

"What?" Tim looked up.

The two figures were up and walking toward the car. It was then that, without them over the object they were carrying, Joana realized what it was. It wasn't a dog at all. It was a child. Left for dead, the two tall aggressors strode toward the car leaving the little boy in the street. The kid wasn't moving. He was just lying there…dead.

"Oh my, God… What do we do?" Joana panicked, watching the two attackers close the distance between them.

They started running toward the car. One of them was holding something. A spear. Tim and Joana watched, while in mid-run, the figure raised the weapon up, lobbing it at the car.

"Drive!" Tim insisted.

The long slender object collided with the hood, scraping against it. The teeth grinding sound of metal scraping against stone reverberated in the street. The spear fell to the gravel beside the car, only the car's paint job damaged.

Joana screamed.

"Fuckin' drive!" Tim shouted, reaching over and shoving her leg down on the gas.

The engine revved, but didn't move. The car was in park.

The two figures running down on them grew closer. Their bare feet slapped across the asphalt with each dashing stride. Close enough now that the cars headlights illuminated them, both Joana and Tim's eyes went wide with disbelief. Those weren't Disney Channel fan-club hats. Those were their ears. They were bears or something like it. But that wasn't possible. They were upright. Walking like humans. Aside from the hair that covered their bodies and face, they were human. Dressed like something Joana would have seen on the Discovery Channel, they were wearing primitive clothing. Rags around their waists, bone necklaces and bracelets. It just didn't make any sense. At least not to—

"Stupid fat bitch! You trying to get us killed? Drive the fuckin' car!" Tim shoved her.

Jarred from her paralyzed state, Joana winced. Who was he calling bitch? She slammed the shifter into drive. The lead attacker lunged on top of the hood, scratching it with his talon-like fingernails. They were long and black… and sharp. Clawing at the car made screeching noises like fingernails to a chalkboard. Only she wasn't in school and that wasn't a chalkboard. It was her car, and she was being attacked from all sides. Tim pushed on her and yelled. With her focus drawn to the figure on the hood, for a split second she forgot all about the second assailant. But she was quickly reminded when it reached the driver's side door and grabbed at her.

Joana kept screaming.

The figured pulled at her with its sharp claws. The sleeve of her shirt ripped. Her shoulder felt warm and wet. The pain was instant.

Fear engrossed, Joana closed her eyes, gripped the steering wheel tightly with both hands, and slammed on the gas. Her lungs bellowed out a loud cry the entire time. While the car raced forward in the street, she screamed. She was even screaming when she felt the arm let go of her from outside. She screamed over Tim's shouting protests. She continued to scream when she felt the car run something over in the street. First it was the front tires. Then the rear. Even with her eyes closed she could see it. She envisioned the little boy, dead in the street, each tire rolling over his dead corpse.

Her screams grew louder. Joana was out of breath, yet the noise still came forth from her empty lungs.

"Slow down!" She thought she heard Tim shout. "Watch out!"

Joana opened her eyes, but it was too late. She yanked the wheel hard to the right just as the front end collided with the side of a parked truck. It all happened so fast. The creature that she thought was a man flew across the hood into the truck, and then disappeared on the other side. The front end of her car pressed in like an accordion. The windshield shattered. The sharp pain in her chest as the air bag engulfed her vision, pressed the back of her head against the seat. The shattered windshield.

Everything stopped and for a moment things went black.

When Joana looked up, still in shock, the airbag was deflated. Steam rose from the crushed front end of her mom's car. The side of the truck she had collided with was even worse off. Her stomach tensed as the thought of explaining all of this to her parents rushed to the surface. Her ears rang. She rubbed her throbbing head and looked to the passenger seat.

Tim was gone.

The first thing she thought of was his seatbelt. He never wore the damn seatbelt. Her mind instantly switched to a different, more terrifying thought. Those *things* in the street. She craned her neck, looking in the rearview mirror. There was no sign of life. Nothing moved. Her eyes did catch a quick glimpse of the small body still lying in the road. The one that she was sure she ran over. Her heart sank and the emotions raced. Confusion. Dizziness. Fear. Regret. Adrenaline surged through her body. The thick mixture of feelings coursed through her, forcing her stomach to churn. She unlatched her safety belt, leaned out the window, and vomited. The warm, wet splash resonated in her ear as the puke plopped across the pavement.

She stopped to catch her breath and wiped her lips. Her throat felt sore.

Something shifted outside the car.

Hearing it, Joana froze, gripped with fear.

"Jooa…"

There it was again. Faint, yet not all that far away. It sounded like Tim. He was hur—

"Joooanna…"

It *was* Tim!

Oh, God. Tim got thrown from the car. He's probably paralyzed, she thought, opening the door and climbing out. Stepping in the still warm vomit, she almost slipped. Not even paying it any mind, her thoughts raced as she rounded the front of her car to investigate. *Oh, please be okay… I should have had my eyes opened. I should have—*

There was Tim lying in the grass on the other side of the truck collision. He was sitting up, thank God. But he looked like he was in a lot of pain. His face was scrunched up and he was holding his side. It looked like he had a pretty good gash on his head.

Blood and thick strands of his long black hair lined the left side of his face.

"Are you okay?" Joana gulped, leaning in to aid him.

He reached out to her. She nodded, helping him to his feet. He groaned out loud as she heaved him up. For a stick, he sure was heavy.

"Oh, God. Please tell me you're okay. I'm so sorry…"

Still gritting his teeth and holding his side with one hand, he was clearly in a lot of pain. He didn't reply. He just pointed. Joana's eyes followed the direction of his shaking hand. When her eyes met the stop he was intending for her to see, she couldn't believe it. What had happened really *had* happened. The bear of a man that was attacking the hood of her mom's car when they crashed was lying on the sidewalk between the parked truck and the closed shops.

It was dead. A large pool of red liquid pooled around its skull.

"Thing…" Tim winced. "Thing cracked its skull wide open when it hit… the sidewalk."

Joana looked closer, confirming her boyfriend's statement to be true.

"What the hell do you… think that is?" Tim continued with a raspy voice. Stepping away from Joana toward the corpse, his eyes went wide. He grimaced while struggling to stand. Falling to his knees, he leaned against the truck that Joana had hit, and said, "I've never seen anything like it. What if we actually… did it, man? Opened up the multi-verse. I can't believe it. We weren't there to see it.

This is it. This is proof. The stones worked. We need to find the rift… and get the hell out of here. It's a door to another world, Joana. We did it. These things… they came from that world. I can feel it."

Tim was full of shit. There was no telling where these things could have come from. Sure as hell wasn't any rift. They had done his stupid little Geomancy trick back at old man Terry's house. And that was nearly a ten minute drive away in the other direction. No way could these things have made it that far on foot. Let alone beat them there with her driving. They could have been living in the mountainside for all they knew. This was all just some big coincidence. What she wanted to say was that they needed to call someone. Get him to the doctor. He was in no shape to be walking around. For Christ's sake, his head was bleeding. She started to speak, but couldn't find the words she was looking for. Instead her hand reached her open mouth, the corpse before them an oddity of nature. What she was seeing couldn't be real.

"What the hell…," Tim stretched his chest out, trying to stand on his own, "were you thinking? Nearly killed me."

Had her mind not jumped to the fact that there had been two of those creatures, she would have snapped at Tim for giving her shit. Even with the chaos and disaster he was too worried about himself to even bother asking if she was all right. Freaking prick.

"Will you help me up?" Tim put a hand up for her, while still leaning against the truck.

"The other one." Joana looked out into the street.

"What?"

"The other one. There was two of them... remember?"

"Oh shit, you're right."

They both looked on.

The street was silent. Still.

After a moment, Joana spoke up, whispering, "We need to call someone. You got your cellphone?"

Tim patted his black jeans down. "Must a fell out of my pocket when I got *flung* from the car."

Joana noticed how Tim made sure to emphasize the getting thrown from the car part. As if all of this was her fault.

"Hey, I was wearing *my* seatbelt."

He rolled his eyes, and then started scanning the ground for his phone. "Couldn't have gone far."

Suddenly the wind picked up. A few parking spots away flickering light caught Joana's attention.

"Look over there." She tapped Tim on the shoulder.

He winced with great agony. Just when he was probably about to jump her shit about grabbing his arm like that, he looked up and saw it too. The light was growing. Pulsing. The purple and blue hues penetrated the darkness, growing larger.

"I'm scared." Joana said.

"That's it..." Tim grinned, forcing himself upright. "One of the rifts. I can't explain how there's one here, opening up miles away from where we did the ritual. But still. That's it. That's what we wanted. Let's go!" He started hobbling toward it.

"Are you out of your mind?" Joana barked, holding him back. "Look. Something's happening."

She was right. Something was happening. Figures much like the ones they had already encountered made their way through the beam of light.

"Let me go." Tim said, trying to pry his way free from her.

She was stronger than him and she knew it. The countless times they had spent wrestling naked in the bed was proof of that. She outweighed him by nearly half.

"You're going to get us killed," she whispered, yanking him away from the truck and toward a narrow alley between two of the small shops.

"No… this is our chance." He protested, trying to wiggle his way free from her arms. "This is what it was all about."

Joana and her boyfriend were quickly out of sight. Tim's words resonated in Joana's mind as they collided into the dark covering the alley provided. Just as the first creature penetrated the rift, *This is what it was all about…* Killer koala bears from another dimension was nowhere near what it was all about. That stupid Geomancy crap was just her way of trying to get Tim out of the house and off that stupid computer. She just wanted them to have more of an active life together. Not this. As it was all happening, she suddenly felt like maybe he was right. The ritual had worked.

Tripping in the darkness, Joana fell backward, the weight of Tim on top of her keeping her from catching her balance. Colliding with what she could only assume was a tin garbage can, it echoed out in the alley like a thundering boom, its contents cascading across the ground.

With her back against the ground and Tim on top of her, she froze silent. Her heart raced and her breathing was heavy. She could tell that Tim really was in a lot of pain, because he was no longer fighting her. Instead he was gripping at his side with both hands just doing his best to breathe. She felt sorry for him and until now had forgotten about her own injuries. Her head throbbed anew, the shoulder where her shirt was torn still bleeding.

"But we can finally escape this place." Tim rasped, out of breath.

"Shh…" Joana shoved a hand over his mouth and listened. "I don't think they heard us come down this—"

Her hopes were instantly shattered. One of the creatures stepped in the alley entrance, looked Joana dead in the eyes, and hissed like a wild animal.

4

The Greenbrier River Valley was changing.

Lewisburg, West Virginia was opening up. All over the small quiet town, seams in the fabric of reality gave birth to a new fate for its humble citizens. More than a hundred rifts had surfaced, spanning the entire valley surrounding the town. Within the hour, it would be flooded with the new invaders from the other side.

The worst had just begun.

Jennifer Blannet awoke to her two boys rushing into her room and jumping on the bed. It was a normal custom at their age. Thunderstorms and the occasional scary movie before bed would generally send them both dashing into her bed at any given time in the middle of the night. The Dark man lurking in their closet or under their bed. With twins at the age of six that shared a room, what else was she to expect? After Jon, her husband, went to Iraq and never came back, things had become tough.

Groggy and confused, she did her best to cling to that last fleeting memory, her dreams taking her back to when Jon was still alive.

"What is it, boys?" Jennifer asked, rubbing sleep from her eyes and pulling the covers back for the boys to climb into bed. She listened for a second to the sounds around them. No thunder. Ushering them under the covers, she said, "Bad dreams?"

"No." Kyle said, the younger of the two by only a few minutes. "The bear-man… it's at the window."

"Oh, come now. There's no such thing." She pleaded with a yawn. "Now let's go back to bed. Mommy was having a good dream about Daddy."

"For real, Momma. There was a bear-man. I saw it, too." Jonny said, pulling on her pajamas. He was named after his father. "Please. You have to go see."

"But it's late, you guys. Can we just go to sleep… please…" She slammed her head back into the pillow and slung one arm up over her eyes. "I'm tired."

"But, Mamma." Kyle pouted, standing up in the bed.

Jennifer felt the bed shift. Trying to ignore it, she groaned and turned to one side.

"I wish Daddy was here." Jonny breathed. "He'd believe us. There really was a bear at our window."

Jennifer's heart sank. She wished Jon was still around, too. She took a deep breath, remembering his face and sighed. Rolling over on her back, she looked at both of the boys. Their expressions were stricken with fear. They really were scared. Seeing them like that made her heart sink even more.

Reaching up, she patted Kyle on the shoulder and spoke with a soothing voice. "It was just a bad dream, boys. Now let's get some sleep. There is no such thing as a bear-man creature, and there was nothing trying to get into your wind—"

Glass shattered from the direction of the boys' room.

Panic set it.

"What was that?" She breathed.

"He's going to eat us."

Both of the boys started crying.

"Umm… get under the bed. Now… just do it!" Jennifer demanded, hearing footsteps drawing toward her room down the hall.

The boys complied with her wishes as she shoved them off the bed. Before she had a chance to climb off the mattress and find a weapon, the intruder was at her door. She gasped from sheer fright and amazement. The size of a grown man, it was covered in grey and white hair. Its muscles flexed beneath the thick coat as it stood there glaring at her with snarling sharp teeth. Drool dripped from its lips like a wild animal hunting prey. Its left shoulder was soaked with something red. The way it breathed through its nose, just huffing and snarling at her made her shrink inside. Like Alice in Wonderland this brutal creature had somehow forced her to eat the cookie just by being in the room.

The boys had been right. It was a bear. She could hear them weeping at her feet beneath the bed.

"Get the hell out of my house!" She yelled, grabbing the lamp from her nightstand.

The cord tore from the wall and a few loose items on the nightstand hit the floor. Startled, she felt the boys jump with fright under the bed.

"Leave us alone. I've already called the cops!"

The beast snarled at her with a wicked grin. One of the large furry gray ears on its head twitched as it looked around the room. The monster was tall, hunched over slightly to fit into the doorway. It reached up licking his paw. That was when Jennifer saw the monstrously sharp black fingernails.

"What do you want? Please just leave…" Her voice wavered, the lamp in her hand shaking.

She was afraid and she knew that this… this *thing* could tell.

"Taem hserf." The creature grinned.

The beast lunged forward. Jennifer screamed, sending the lamp flying. Her attacker batted it away in midair falling on her with both paws clawing. Ravenous and wild with rage, the monster slashed at her with his sharp claws. The utter weight of the creature forced Jennifer to the floor. Trying to fight her way free, Jennifer lifted up an arm to avoid getting slashed in the face. Her arm received the brunt of the pain instead. With one fast swipe the deep lacerations from the monster's claws sent crimson flowing.

Jennifer Blannet's screams of agony filled the air, her boys left under the bed to watch her sufferings.

The bear continued to slice and claw at her with his sharp paws. Grunting with delight and hunger, the arm that she had been blocking with fell to the floor, severed. The creature's claws were so sharp that after only a few fierce strikes, it was able to separate the bone. Blood pooled around her as she cried out. The shouts seemed to excite her attacker even more. With her arm no longer in the way, her face was next. With one wide slice, three claw marks tore at the skin of her beautiful face. The pain was excruciating. Jamming its claws deep, she felt her right eye burst. She tried to scream again, but her cries were cut short by gurgling and choking. Blood and plasma had run down from the pulpous eye and into her mouth. Gagging on her own sinew and gore gave her no quarter from the creature. It sliced at her pajamas. It grunted and hissed as blood and cotton cupcakes shredded away like grated cheese.

Her life was drained. She had no fight left. She lay ready to accept this strange fate. She turned her neck toward the bed and coughed. Blood jutted from her lips and leaked from an empty eye socket. She saw her severed arm lying there beside her bleeding all over the carpet, soaking in deep.

The creature stopped slicing at her for a moment and in the peripheral of her one good eye, she saw it pulling a small dagger from the cloth on its hip. Ignoring it, a lone tear ran down her face as she finally looked past her severed arm at the boys still tucked away under the bed. Their eyes were locked with one another. She had never seen them more terrified in all her life. Holding each other tight, she watched them quiver and cry. She wanted to reach out, hold their hands. Tell them it would all be okay. That she would protect them. That she was going to be with Daddy now. And that it was all okay.

When she opened her mouth to say these things only blood flowed.

The pain was even sharper than before. It was like her stomach had exploded. She looked up suppressing the pain. Her eye was sealed on the intruder and what it was doing to her. After slicing her wide open, it reached in with its bear-like paw and began to feast.

Jennifer was dead before the first warm morsel reached its lips.

That was when Kyle could be quiet no more. He cried out for his father. Daddy would protect them if he would just come home.

Their location was compromised.

The koala bear grinned, the intestinal muck dripping from its lips.

There was more to eat.

The Blannet family wasn't the only one having trouble tonight. It was happening all over town.

Ben Pepperstien, Jenifer's next door neighbor, heard the shouting and screaming. Had he already been to bed he might have slept right through it. But he was more of a night owl and went outside to investigate. He normally worked third shift at the local grocery store stocking the shelves at night while the store was closed. Tonight he had called in, not because he was sick or had important plans. He had just called in because he hated his job. The only good thing about that place was the fact that they didn't have any surveillance cameras. During lunch break, he and some of the other co-workers wouldn't worry about packing a lunch. It was a grocery store. There was always plenty to choose from.

With a fresh can of ice-cold beer in hand and bathrobe over his otherwise naked body, Ben didn't even make it two feet onto his front porch. His eyes caught a quick glimpse of something darting past him in the dark and that was it.

His head rolled off, separating from the rest of his body. It hit the porch and rolled a few feet into the grass before the beer ever slipped from his hand.

The humanoid bear that had delivered the deathblow rejoiced with a triumphant animal-like roar of victory. It stuffed the sharp sliver of bone covered in the dead man's blood back into its sheath, not bothering to wipe away the gore. Stepping over to the severed head, it picked the thing up and licked at the leaking substance running from the human's neck. Satisfied, it bit into the meaty tissue and tossed the head to the ground. A thick coat of bloody filth stained its fur.

Gulping down the thick salty meat, the creature grunted at another of its kind. They both grabbed at one of the dead man's legs and dragged it from the porch out into the street. When they reached the pulsing beam of light nearby, the two hungry koala bears pulled the headless body through the portal and into their world.

Minutes later, the two bears returned, leaving the body behind.

Pete, Tim and Joana's friend, was masturbating to some old VHS porn tapes from the 60's when he was interrupted. Not by the fact that both of his dogs where in the back yard barking like there was no tomorrow. No, he was ignoring them. Every now and again a skunk or something would pass by stirring up trouble with the dogs. It was worse. His dad practically kicked his bedroom door down while he was in middle of his business. Pete jumped covering himself with the blanket, the video still playing on the TV in his room, the volume off so as to keep from waking his old man. His dad was a cranky fuck when people disturbed his rest.

"Shit, Dad. Ever heard of knocking?" Pete said, picking up the remote and turning off the TV before the old mad had a chance to see. His face was beet red.

"Put your dick in your pants, boy. Somethin's happenin' outside. Haven't you heard all that racket?"

"So what? The dogs bark through the night all the time." Pete said, trying to not seem embarrassed.

"No, listen." His dad paused for a second. "Someone is gettin' shot at."

"I don't hear anything," Pete said, reaching for a pair of pants and putting them on while still under the covers.

"Shh…" His dad lifted a hand to his lips.

It was then that Pete realized that his dad had one of his guns out. That meant he was being serious. Pete listened a moment longer and before he could protest once more about his old man respecting his privacy, his dad interrupted him.

"Here, take this." His dad tossed the gun at him. "Put on your shoes. We need to go see what the hell is goin' on out there."

"Can't you just call the cops or something?" It was too late. His dad had already disappeared from the doorway, apparently going back into the bedroom for another gun.

As he finished getting dressed, his mind raced with the idea that his old man had just walked in on him doing the you-know-what. He shook his head, tying his shoes and picking the gun up from the bed. This time tomorrow afternoon he wasn't sure he'd be able to look his dad in the eyes with a straight face. He just hoped that his mom wasn't going to end up hearing about it.

Pete followed his dad out the back door where the dogs were still barking. Had there not been a single cloud in the sky it might have been pitch black outside. But with no clouds in sight, the moon was shining bright. At first his eyes had to adjust, but in under a minute he was able to see very well in the darkness.

The dogs were in their pens freaking the fuck out. They were barking at something to the east side of the house. Pete's dad nodded at him and walked off. His dad was like that. Thought just because he was a gun enthusiast that he was some kind of Rambo or some shit. Pete half expected his dad to do some crazy hand signals that meant some operative sneak maneuver or something. He didn't. Instead, he disappeared around the side of the house, slow stepping his way toward the front.

Pete shrugged, stepped over to the dog cage, and tried to calm them. It wasn't working. They were vicious. Whatever was out there definitely had them spooked. Opening the cage to usher them into the house, he got knocked on his ass. Both of the dogs bolted from their cage, pushing past him, and running off.

"Fuck…" Pete said, standing up and wiping dirt from his rear.

The dogs were gone. That was when he heard the first shot fired. The report reverberated off the houses around him. It was hard to tell where it was coming from.

Another shot rang out.

"Dad!" It was coming from the front of the house.

Pete ran around the side of the house in the direction that his dad had gone. When he reached the front yard, he stopped, paralyzed with incredulity.

It was a warzone. There were nearly 10 houses on his block and every single one had something happening. The front door to the neighbor's house across the street was wide open. A tall man in a hairy bear suit was pulling his neighbor out the front door and into the street. The neighbor to the right was in his yard swinging a tennis racket at two figures wearing the same crazy outfits. They were stabbing at him. Killing him. Screams filled his ears. His eyes went wide and his mouth dropped. The house to his left was on fire. It wasn't fully engulfed, but he could see the yellow bursts of heat dancing around inside through one of the windows.

In the street, one of the men wearing a bear suit was straddling someone. He drove a sharp object into their chest over and over again while sitting on top of him. The person receiving the blows wasn't moving. Right next to the body was a gun. Pete's dad's gun.

Pete screamed.

The spear went straight through his heart before Pete ever even had the chance to see the creature that threw it.

One couple had been up all night arguing about finances when their home was overrun. The man managed to take a few of them out with a baseball bat before being harpooned in the face. His wife screamed witnessing it all as he did what he could to protect her. With him no longer there to defend her they were on her in seconds producing a much more gruesome act of violence against her than her husband. She was still alive when they started to eat her.

Across town some people didn't even get as much warning. Still in their beds dead asleep, they were soon just dead. Violence filled the night.

War broke out in the streets as every other home was looted for fresh meat. Screams and gunfire filled the Greenbrier River Valley.

5

Joana saw the purple strips of her hair bouncing about in front of her face as she ran, pulling Tim along as best as she could.

"Oh my God, we're dead. They're going to kill us." She panted, trying to catch her breath.

Tim didn't reply. His heaves of pain from each charging step were a constant reminder for Joana. With each grunt her mind replayed the train wreck of events. Tim was lucky to be alive. He had been thrown from the car, for crying out loud. She was thankful things hadn't turned out worse.

Ha! She laughed at that thought. *Worse…*

It couldn't get any worse than this. They were being chased by something out of a freaking 80's B-film. Those had been her favorite times spent with her deadbeat boyfriend; snuggled up on the couch in front of the TV watching movies like *Killer Clowns from Outerspace* and *Trimmers*. For a split second, she thought she could smell the popcorn; heard it popping in the microwave.

Her hopes were dashed.

Dead end. The alley ended.

Forced to stop, Joana leaned against the unanticipated blockade trying to catch her breath. She was out of shape and she knew it. She had Tim to remind her all the damn time.

Those popping sounds hadn't been the sweet savory flavors of butter flavored kernels. It had been footsteps giving chase, bouncing off either side of the walls in the alley.

They had been lucky the first time, but now… now they were fucked.

"Why'd we stop?" Tim groaned, leaning over.

Joana looked past him down the alley, then back his way.

His hand stuck to his side like superglue. She was no doctor, but it was likely that he had cracked ribs. She had gotten one or two of those before. They're bearable, but very painful. The more you moved the more it hurt. The more it hurt, the more uncomfortable you were… so you moved. It was a vicious cycle. The side of his face was caked with blood. Luckily the bleeding on his head had stopped, forming a deep red crust. There was no telling how bad the cut, or cuts, were. With that much blood there was no way he didn't need a few stitches. Then again, she was no doctor. She wanted to be a baker. Have her own baking show. Sweets were her passion.

"I said, why the fuck did we stop?" Tim grunted, looking around her round frame at the brick wall blocking their path.

The sounds of popping corn coming up the alley reminded her of the immediate threat. Her mind was like that. It wandered when she was nervous or scared, and right now, she was both. A wild growl howled in the distance. When she looked past Tim, her teeth slammed shut almost biting her tongue. Several bear-like shadows stretched out across the alley's floor and walls. They were gaining on them.

"What do we do?"

It would be only a matter of seconds before those monsters were on them. Killing them. Eating them.

Or worse. A flash of what was to come jarred her from the situation, her mind leaving Tim all alone once more. The creatures reached them. Taking Tim first, Joana was left cowering in the corner of the alley balling her eyes out as she watched them make Tim suffer. In her mind's eye it made her feel better that Tim had to suffer first. That scared her. Tim had been holding her back and she was about to pay the price for it. Maybe she didn't care for him as much as she thought she had. Maybe she was just a selfish bitch and that's why no one else but Tim really liked her. Maybe Tim cared for her more and he wasn't the problem in the relationship. It was too late a life lesson for her to benefit now.

A hand reached out and jerked Joana back to reality. A reality much more horrifying than her wildest nightmares.

"In here!" Tim yelled between gritting teeth and discomfort.

Joana crashed into something. She lost her balance and fell flat in the darkness. Her hands slapped hard on the floor as she protected her face.

A door slammed behind her making her jump. She spun around and climbed to her feet. With it hard to see in the dark she half expected gnashing teeth or a sharp set of claws slicing into her already sore shoulder. Her eyes adjusted to the light as something heavy scraped across the floor. Tim grunted behind it.

"Help me!"

Tim was pushing a small couch in front of the door, and having hell of a time at it. If his wounds from the crash weren't enough to keep him from moving the furniture, his small size was. Joana jumped in to help. The second the couch pressed in front of the door they fell silent, listening to the nothingness around them.

Faint grunts and hisses met their ears after a moment. The creatures giving chase had reached the end of the alley. Joana began to panic, breathing heavier than before. Tim lifted the black painted fingernail of his index finger to his lips.

"Shhh…"

She cupped her mouth with her hand as they both leaned against the couch. From the sound of it, there was quite a few of them out there. A sudden metallic *boom* slammed against the wall outside followed by faint rustling noises. *They* were looking for them.

Joana started to get up, but Tim shook his head. She stopped and settled back into the couch staying quiet.

Then she realized something. Tim had just saved her life. Fate was giving them a second chance. The boy she had slowly been growing to hate really was a man after all. He had protected her. Been her knight in shining armor. She locked gazes with him in the dim light of the store. His eyes glistened. She had been thinking the wrong things lately. Taking relationship advice from the wrong people. Hell, it was all making sense now. Their relationship hadn't started to suffer until she started listening to Mina Jones at school. She breathed a heavy sigh of relief.

The noises outside faded. The would-be assaulters had gone.

"What the fuck were you thinking out there, stupid bitch?" Tim stood up, finally breaking the silence. "You could-a got us killed!"

Then it all flooded back to the surface. There was a reason she was seeking advice about their problems. He had become an asshole.

"One minute, you're crashing your mom's car. The next, giving me fucking whiplash dragging me down the damn alley. Then when we're actually in danger getting chased…" Tim stopped, making a pain filled face while gripping his ribs. "When we're actually getting chased… you space out on me and just stand there. What the hell, Joana?"

"Look who's talking." Joana pulled herself from the couch and looked around.

The room was some type of office. If her memory was correct, they were in a surplus store for outdoor equipment. Posters of people canoeing, rock climbing, and hiking lined the walls. Aside from the couch they had moved, there was one large desk with a computer, with lots of papers and boxes beside it. There was one other door, which undoubtedly led into the storefront. She had visited it once or twice with her dad before going fishing. This was where her dad got his bait and stuff.

"And what the hell does that mean? Look who's talking… what?" Tim tossed a hand in the air. "I have blood all over the side of my fa—"

"Just shut up, Tim. Dear God. What the hell did you get us into here?"

"Me… what do you mean, me? I'm not the one that trashed the car and dragged us down here."

"You're telling me," Joana stepped forward, two fingers in Tim's face. "You didn't see those things out there. They were bears that were human, Tim. Human bears! Where the hell did they come from, huh?"

"I don't know…" Tim stepped back.

"What the hell do you mean 'you don't know'? I'm not the one that almost got you killed. If anything, I saved your ass back there."

"By what… spacing out on me?"

"No, by pulling you into the alley to begin with. Or did you forget that part already?"

"What the hell are we even talking about?" Tim protested, leaning against the computer desk.

Joana shook her head, ran her fingers through her hair, and sighed. After a deep breath, she calmed, and said, "Before we ran down the alley you said something. You said this was it. Our chance to leave. That the stupid stones worked. How do you know that for sure?"

"I didn't say that."

Joana put both fists on her wide hips and glared.

"Look… we don't know anything for sure. Okay. All I know is I was told it would work. We just wanted to leave. Go somewhere better."

"No…" Joana hissed. "You wanted to leave. I never said I did. I like it here."

An unexpected look slid across Tim's face. He seemed shocked and at a loss for words. He just stood leaning against the desk, blood caked on his face along with that smug expression.

"None of that matters, all right?" Joana said, her voice soothing. "We need to get out of here. Call the cops or something."

Tim nodded.

With that, Tim braced himself, and then stepped away from the desk. Joana opened the door leading into the store and followed Tim as he limped ahead, one hand on his side. She felt sorry for him regardless of whose fault it all was.

"The register's up at the front." Joana whispered, grabbing Tim's hand for comfort. "Maybe there's a phone up there.

Tim nodded, slowly easing them in that direction.

The entire front of the store was made of glass so those that passed by on the street could peer in at the many outdoor selections inside. The wall was adorned with a few small kayaks and fishing gear. A small child's tent was set up at the front. A fake fire pit and a few chairs surrounded the entrance of the tent for demonstration.

Looking beyond the front window, no strange activity was happening on the street. As they drew closer, Joana saw her mom's car still pressed against the parked truck. The wreck had happened right in front of the outdoor store. Her stomach tightened at the sight. Her mom loved that car.

"Here it is," Tim breathed.

They reached the counter. Tim was sifting through some things behind it. Joana wasn't watching him. Her gaze was fixated on what was outside. She couldn't look away. She just knew, that like the countless horror movies that she had watched with Tim, something was going to jump out… slam into the glass scaring her senseless. Her heart raced just waiting for that moment. She longed for it to get over with.

"Got it!" Tim said, a hint of excitement mixed in there with the painful grunt.

Joana jumped.

Tim laughed, instantly regretting it with a painful wince.

"Serves you right. That wasn't funny. You scared the shit out of me." She looked down at the phone in Tim's hand.

"Had to figure out how to dial out."

"Awesome." Joana said, watching him dial 911 before returning her focus to the street.

"Great."

"What?" Joana asked, not taking her eyes away from the window.

"Line's busy."

"Well, do we know the actual number to the local police?"

Just as those words left her lips, a flash of red and blue lights saturated the street beyond the store. Joana heard Tim hang the phone up. They both watched in horror as the patrol car eased past with its lights flashing. There were two of those monsters already on the hood of the car trying to get in. The windshield shattered, and just like that, the cruiser eased up onto the sidewalk slamming into a fire hydrant across the street. The hydrant shifted from its stoop and water gushed forth like Old Faithful. The creatures attacking the car didn't stop. No shots were fired. No cops got out of the car kicking asses and taking names. No, the bears climbed down from the car, dragging two very dead cops into the street.

Tim whimpered and ducked down low behind the counter. Joana felt him shift beside her and did likewise, dropping low, but to where she could still see what was happening outside.

They were eating.

They were tearing the cops' clothing with their claws and eating the bodies.

Joana suddenly didn't feel so great.

Two more figures walked into view. More of the same bear-people. Seeing the spoils set out before the ones feasting, the two newcomers looked to gain a portion of the pillage. One of the two already eating shooed them away.

Blood stained the street.

"What are we going to do? How are we supposed to get out of here?" Joana whined.

"I don't know." Tim said, stepping out from behind the counter and putting an arm around her. "Right now, we just need to sit tight. Try the phone a few more times. Someone will answer."

"Yeah…" Joana cried, leaning into his scrawny chest.

Joana had seen enough.

He held her tight, the sounds of feasting and slurping grunts penetrating the thick glass of the outdoor store.

6

Frank Edelman's blood ran down his arm from the wound in his shoulder into the sink. With both hands on either side of the bowl, he leaned against the counter staring at himself in the mirror— preparing himself. Building up the courage to do it. He was just thankful that he was slowly regaining mobility in that hand, not matter how much it hurt to move his shoulder.

He had already snapped the loose wooden spear wedged in his shoulder past the flesh. As if that hadn't been painful enough, causing the blood to flow anew, now he had nothing to hold onto when pulling the rest of the object out of his arm.

The room smelled of bleach, a result of him going overboard with the cleaning for tomorrow's art opening. The fumes made his eyes burn, which was why he had the door open. The light overhead flickered slightly. Frank gritted his teeth each time the darkness jumped forward. He had just changed that damn bulb, too. The sound of water rushing from the faucet and down the drain echoed off the tile floor and marble walls in the one person bathroom.

Nodding at himself in the mirror, he was ready.

He needed to get this thing out of his arm, stop the bleeding, and get to Kathie before it was too late.

After those creatures left that man lying in the street half eaten, Frank tried calling Kathie a few more times. The line was busy. It was busy when he called 911 as well. Frustrated, he pocketed the phone. While deciding what to do, he watched the creatures return and then drag the partially devoured corpse away. For a minute, he thought about making a run for it. His vehicle was just right there. He would be across town and to Kathie in less than 15 minutes. But when he stepped forward and reached for the door, the sharp pain was too much. With his focus largely on getting to Kathie he had somehow forgotten about the shoulder. Sharp jolting stabs ran down his arm and through his hand. The pain was so intense that Frank dropped to one knee, gripping at his shoulder with his left hand. His left hand came away red. The pain finally subsided. He looked back out to the street.

There were more of them out there. Scavenging, it looked like.

If he were going to make a run for it he needed to do so something about that shoulder.

That was when he found himself in the bathroom.

By now, at least 10 minutes had passed. On the toilet lid was a bottle of peroxide, two clean towels to stop the bleeding, some bandage wrap from the first aid kit in the office, and some duct tape. With each minute that passed, his heart sank even more. Kathie needed him.

And, Captain… his dog, his best friend was… dead.

He couldn't stand it anymore. He had to act.

Jamming his left hand into his right shoulder, the index finger, middle finger, and thumb went to work. Blood rushed from his wound as the three fingers tore flesh around the small spear's sharp tip.

"Fuuucc…" Frank bit down hard, his eyes watering.

Just when he was about to give up, he got hold of it and pulled. Drool and spit dripped from his lips between clenched teeth as the sharp stone cut though muscle inside his shoulder. He moaned while fighting through the pain.

He dropped the arrow head in the sink. It clinked to a rest near the drain. The arrow head was covered in blood.

He sighed with a bit of relief. The brunt of the pain was over.

He'd never doctored anyone up before, but he had a general idea of what to do. The peroxide stung when he poured it over the open gash. He watched at the gaping hole in his shoulder, the size of a quarter, fizzed with white foam. The liquid was doing its job.

Bandaged up with what he had available, Frank left the bathroom and went back out to investigate the parking lot. He zipped up his coveralls while passing toward the door, not even bothering to rinse his blood out of the sink. With wide stretched steps, he was there in half the time it normally took. The lot looked empty.

He pulled out the phone and keys and dialed Kathie one last time for good measure. Busy signal—again. Either the lines were jammed with a flood of calls or the lines were down all together. He hung up and dialed 911 just to see. With the phone to his ear, he scanned the lot, and used his right hand to unlock the door. He was able to use his right hand, but it definitely didn't feel pleasant.

The parking lot seemed empty enough.

He went for it.

With his phone in one hand and the keys in his other, he thought of turning to lock the door. He didn't care. There was no time for that.

The door swung open and Frank darted toward the white 1982 GMC Jimmy. His eyes shifted hard to the left, and then to the right. He saw the mangled remains of what had been that man those creatures had eaten and dragged off to God-knows-where. The pavement was stained with a large portion of blood. Rank chunks of meaty stuff lay scattered around it, parts the monsters had missed or discarded during the feast. Frank didn't want to think about it and looked away.

He was almost home free.

Only a few feet from the car, he heard something start to give chase off to his left. An odd series of noises erupted in that direction, a language maybe. He didn't look. He didn't want to know how many there where. Just as he reached the door, jamming the car key into place, he felt something wiz past his ear. Just as the gust of wind whooshed by, the sound of wood dropped to the cement near his feet.

They were throwing spears at him.

He yanked the door open and jumped into the vehicle. The driver side door's window shattered. Just before Frank yanked the door closed, he had watched the slender object crash through. Broken glass fell in his lap as the door slammed shut. He cranked the car and looked up. His gold and green senior tassel was draped from the rearview mirror. But that's not what he was looking at.

There were five of them, all bearing down on him with anger and malice. Another spear flew past the windshield.

"Fuck you, motherfuckers!" Frank crammed the shifter into drive and slammed the accelerator to the floor.

The Jimmy jumped forward, taking a split second to catch traction. When it did, the car bolted forward toward the hair-covered attackers. Frank gripped the wheel and turned toward them with intent. Two of the creatures jumped away just in time. The others weren't as lucky.

He braced for impact, felt the car jerk hard toppling over one of them while he watched another slam into his windshield before disappearing over the hood.

He didn't stop. Keeping the gas pedal to the floor he compensated the wheel and got himself realigned toward the street.

His school tassel swayed with each sharp pull of the wheel.

"I love you, baby." Frank said, easing up on the gas to a more manageable speed. "I'm comin' home. Just hang tight."

Tim slammed the phone down.

"The damn thing is still busy!" Tim shouted, the sound of the police siren clearly getting on his last nerve.

Joana had never seen him look this worried in all their time together. Just seeing him like that made her weary and even more afraid than she already was. He was normally the calm, cool, and collected type. Right now, he was none of those. He darted out from behind the register's counter and started walking away back toward the back of the store.

Joana looked back out to the street then at Tim, who was walking away.

"Where the hell are you going?" Joana's said with a pleading voice.

The front area of the store near the register was still illuminated in a hue or red and blue flashing patrol car lights. Now, aside from the totaled cruiser and her mom's pulverized car in the street, there was nothing.

Right after they watched that cop crash his car and then both of the men in blue get dragged out and eaten, a few things happened. Shortly after their little feast on the two cops, Joana and Tim watched the humanoid bears drag the two lifeless corpses across the street toward the swirling rift. A few cars drove by at ungodly speeds, not bothering to stop. Joana didn't blame them one bit. She wanted to get home, make sure her mom and dad were okay, and get the hell out of town. That was probably where those other cars had been headed. Checking on their loved ones or skipping fucking Dodge.

Joana didn't want to think about what was on the other side of that portal.

"Hey…" Joana said, finding confidence. "I asked you a question."

Tim turned to her. "We can't get a hold of anybody. We need to do something. We can't just sit here."

"Well, I'm all for getting the piss out of town, but I sure as shit ain't walking out there." She threw a thumb up over her shoulder toward the front of the store.

Tim just looked at her, and then went back to digging through the rack of outdoor supplies on the shelf.

"Will you talk to me, please? I need you right now. Show a little compassion and just explain what the hell you're doing… what you plan to do."

"Look!" Tim slammed both fists into the shelf, the rack of canoe paddles shook. "I don't know… okay. I'm just looking. That's all."

Joana lowered her head, ready to cry.

"It'll be all right. I promise." Tim said, not even taking the time to look at her. "There's got to be something in here we can use for protection."

"Like weapons?"

"Yes… *like a weapon*." Tim said with a sarcastic inflection. "Now quit standing there and help me look… please."

Joana rolled her eyes, then just dropped the subject and started searching with him. All she wanted was an embrace. A little comfort. To know that he actually cared. But she should have known better than to expect that from him, because the last time he had proved all he really cared about was himself.

"What are we going to do once we find something useful in here? I don't want to back out there."

"We're gonna have to." Tim said, stepping away from the shelf with a machete in hand. "Now that's what I'm talkin' about."

He grinned, taking it out of the package, and then swinging it for good measure.

"Hey, watch out with that damn thing." Joana stepped back so as to not get sliced by accident.

"Hey, there's another one up here if you want it."

She nodded, and Tim handed her the one he had already opened.

Grabbing the other one down and opening the package it was in, he said, "I'm thinking we can sneak out the back if we're quiet enough."

"And go back into the alley?"

"Yeah…" Tim nodded, setting his machete down on the shelf and loosening his belt to slip the sheath on. "When I pulled you in here I noticed a ladder going to the roof and the building across from this one. If we can get on the roof, maybe we can get a better idea of what's happening around us."

"Then what?"

"Well… then we get the fuck out of town before the field closes and…" He cleared his throat. "I mean, before we get killed or something."

"Before the *field* what…"

"Nothing… its nothing." Tim retrieved the machete from the shelf and stuffed it in the sheath on his hip. "Here, let me help you with yours."

"No…" She said, pushing him away as he stepped forward to help her put on a sheath like he had done. "What fucking field… what are you talking about? Don't pretend like you don't know something. What the hell is going on?"

"Okay… look." Tim stepped back and threw both hands in the air. "I knew the rifts were going to open up all over town. All right, I said it. But the bears. I didn't know anything about that. I had no idea it would open up both ways like that. Let alone what would be on the other side. It's not my fault. You should just be happy it worked. We can get out of here."

"I already told you. I never wanted to leave. Now quit dancing around it and tell me everything. What else do you know that you haven't said?"

"Well, now you don't have any choice but to leave. Either by going through one of those portals or by skipping town. And from the looks of those crazy fucks covered in fur outside…," he pointed. "The rift idea is out of the question. That would be suicide. But we need to figure out what's going on out there. The sooner we leave the better."

"And why is that?" Joana bit her lip.

"Because…" Tim swallowed hard. Joana watched as his Adam's apple bobbed up and down on that scrawny neck. "Those stones didn't just open up the rifts. It's closing up around us at the same time. The more of those things that open, the faster it's going to happen."

"I don't understand."

"Think of a dome." Tim waved his hands in the shape of a rainbow. "Nothing can get in and nothing can get out. And it's going to be like that until all those rifts close back up."

"And when the hell were you planning to mention all of this?"

"I didn't think it really mattered." Tim shook his head, shoving his long black hair off of his neck. "We were leaving, remember. I don't give a shit what happens to this dumb little town. Soon as one of those things opened, I was leaving. Remember? We were leaving."

"So you were okay with all of the people we grew up with getting killed as long as you were able to get away?" Joana shouted, pointing a finger in his face.

"I didn't plan all of this. I swear. I had no idea the Arktos was a real freaking creature!"

"You knew—"

A loud thunderous boom out in the street made them both jump in their skin. Out in the street two vehicles collided with one another head on. One was a red pickup truck, the other an ambulance with its lights flashing. Smoke and steam rose from the center of the wreck and Joana heard Tim gasp. She did the same as they watched with grief stricken terror. No one was climbing out of either vehicle. Had any one of them had time to climb out, that's about all the time they would have had. More than ten Arktos' descended on the wreck within seconds. From all sides they fell on the vehicles, some wielding spears, others brandishing large rocks, which they used to smash the glass in.

Screams of pain filled the street as those trapped inside were dragged from the wreckage and devoured on site.

"Wow…" Tim said, his eyes wide.

"I think I'm going to be sick." Joana turned away, unable to stand the gruesome sight.

"We need to leave anyway." Tim patted her on the shoulder. "With all of them busy with the crash we have a better chance getting to the roof unnoticed. But if we're going… then we need to go."

Joana lunged into Tim's chest, wrapping her arms around him tight. "I'm sacred, Tim."

"It'll be alright." Tim hugged her back, hard and long. "I love you."

"I… I love you… too, Tim." She wiped a tear from her cheek.

Tim nodded, forcing her to let go, then they made for the back door.

7

Joana and Tim watched the busy streets below from the safety of the rooftop.

When they hit the alley, it was empty. They didn't waste any time and climbed the ladder to the top. The climb was easy for Tim, even with his side hurting the way it was. Joana watched him climb and was surprised that despite his injury it didn't seem to have slowed him down any. She wondered if he was really in as much pain as he claimed. Joana was more out of breath when they reached the top than Tim.

Joana reached her hand out for Tim to help once she reached the roof. It didn't surprise her this time when she didn't get the assist. Tim glanced at her momentarily and turned his attention to the streets below.

Unbelievable, she thought, forcing her foot up beyond the comfort zone and she climbed onto the roof on her own.

The small two-story building they found themselves on, right next to the outdoor sports outlet, was littered with beer cans, beer bottles, cigarette butts, and a few stray used condoms. Whoever had been hanging out up here had partied hard more than just a few times and not bothered to clean up. Either that, or the one time they did party it was one hell of a night.

The air was cold. The wind blew slightly from the east.

From that height, they could see the calamity happening around them. Keeping low so as to not be seen themselves, they walked around on the roof as quietly as they could. Joana felt uneasy with every step she took, the loose gravel under her feet crunched so loud she winced at each step. Tim didn't seem to notice. She watched him take each step, the rocks under his feet flooding her ears with a sensory overload. Before she had the chance to bring up that they might need to walk a little softer, Tim pointed out into the street.

"Look... What do you think they're doing?" Tim whispered.

Joana ducked low, hugging the guardrail beside her boyfriend. She felt the rolls of fat in her midsection folding over her shirt, creasing it into her gut. In any normal circumstance, she would have sat up straight and pulled her shirt out. This was definitely no normal circumstance. With her hands against the 3' brick wall, her head poked up just enough for her eyes to scan the street. She couldn't believe what she was seeing. She didn't reply to Tim's pervious question. She just watched. There was nothing else she could do.

Below them, where her mom's car set smashed into the parked truck, the ambulance lights and the cruiser lights mixed to brighten the night with an eerie glow. The hydrant that the cruiser had bumped still spewed into the sky. Screams filled the air amidst the sound of the rushing water. They watched for a moment as the paramedics and passengers in the other car met their fate. It was a carnal blood bath, their unmoving bodies lying in the street.

These creatures were relentless. Fearless and filled with rage.

One of the several animal men had knelt down over one of the paramedic bodies. It was hard to see because it had its back turned to the building, but it looked like it was chewing on a severed arm. That was when Tim pointed at something else. Another one of those things walked up to the one eating on the dismembered arm and tried snatching it away. A fight broke out, each shouting in a language that neither Tim nor Joana could understand. The larger of the two bear-like creatures shoved the other to the ground, taking the meaty blood soaked appendage for itself.

Joana couldn't bear to watch. She turned her gaze away, her eyes working their way down long narrow road.

Farther down the road, a white GMC Jimmy roared down the side street. It was in and out of view in an instant. Joana was surprised to have even seen it pass by at all. For a second she thought it looked familiar. In a town this small she knew just about everyone relatively close to her age.

Just as she was about to rattle off a name that might belong to the GMC, Tim pulled her along to check out what was happening on the other side of the buildings.

This side of the building overlooked one of the larger local playgrounds. Swings, merry-go-rounds, slides, a big sand box, and miniature rock climbing sets were scattered across the clean-cut grass. Beyond that was a basketball court with four goals; two on either side. None of the park's lights were on. They were automated, set to go off at 9pm. Joana knew that because she and Tim used to visit the park at night back when they first started dating. They would spend all night out there on the swings just talking, getting to know one another. Back then she felt like she had known him her whole life. Now she wasn't sure if she knew him at all.

At the back of the building, in the park, things seemed a lot calmer. Looking close enough, and forcing her eyes to see far out into the darkness of the playground, she saw a few of the crazy-bears walking around. It was as if they were hunting. They stabbed at the thick bushes as if expecting someone to jump out of hiding. They climbed into the tube-slides from the bottom up. With how they moved, she could tell that all of this was an unfamiliar world to them. Their actions were cautious and highly on alert. Even still, there were a lot less of them on this side and the important thing was that no one was getting eaten down there.

"I think we can make it on this side." Tim said.

"Are you out of your mind? There are bears down there!" She breathed between gritting teeth, not wanting to leave the safety of the roof, despite the fact that she knew he was right. She had just been thinking the same thing.

Tim scanned the grounds and then pointed.

When Joana's eyes followed his hand and landed on what he saw, she wished she hadn't looked.

A woman ran across the playground in full sprint headed toward the basketball court. She wasn't wearing any shoes or pants. Her shirt was torn to shreds. Even in the darkness and from that distance, Joana could see one of her beasts was exposed. It bounced violently up and down as she ran. Once her screams reached the top of the building, the Arktos, as Tim had called it, came into view. Wild and ravenous, it gave chase with long strides that matched the fleeing woman. As it ran, its large rounded fur covered ears laid back to the side of his head. It reminded Joana of what a cat looked like when it was being protective, hissing for you to leave it alone. The woman stumbled, fell to her knees and cried out. She didn't give up. She sprawled forward, regaining her footing and started running again.

Joana's eyes darted from the creature to the woman and back to the creature again. She wanted desperately to shout. Tell the woman not to look back and to keep going. Tell that damn koala looking motherfucker to leave her alone. But she didn't. Fear gripped her and she was thankful that it wasn't her being chased.

The Arktos stopped dead in its tracks.

Joana sighed a heavy fit of relief. It was giving up. *She has a chance. The woman was going to get away. That means we have a chance. We can outrun them.*

Her heart sank when she realized what was actually happening. The bear didn't give up on the chase. No. It was merely done running.

The Arktos pulled a sling from a bag tied to its hip. With the three rocks swirling over the creature's head, it held onto the rope waiting for the right moment to release. Joana's eyes went wide. The faster the rocks spun, something else started to happen. A light emitted from them like some type of tracer. The blue light was like the tail of a comet, spinning with the rotation of the rocks, waiting to catch up to its source.

"We need to do something…"

Tim didn't reply.

How could he? She knew there was nothing they could do to help that poor woman.

And that was when it happened. The sling left the grizzly creature's grip. A long stream of blue light followed the rock as it soared through the air at a rapid pace. Joana heard the rope whizzing in the air as it flung across the darkness hitting its target. The woman groaned, falling face first in the grass. The man-bear charged forward grunting happily.

When the Arktos reached the immobilized woman, her cry of pain shrieked across the night's cool westbound wind.

Joana didn't want to see it. She didn't want to see the carnage. She slumped low, leaning against the wall of the roof and covered her ears. The machete sheathed on her hip leaned awkwardly as she sat. There was no way they were going to get out of this. There were too many of them. They were too fast. They had weapons. Her eyes welled up with fearful tears. When she looked up to Tim to find comfort, something else was wrong.

Tim looked as if he were almost glowing. His skin started to look like a tint of orange.

"Tim. Look at your arm." She pointed, and then realized her arm looked like that, too.

Everything around them, the sky, their skin, the building, and the playground, were all starting to change color. An ominous hue or faint orange was starting to fall over everything like a colored lens filter. Joana thought of the yellow safety glasses her dad had sitting in the visor of his pickup truck. He used them when he went skeet shooting and Joana had gotten a kick out of how they made everything change colors.

Only now, she wasn't getting a kick out of this.

Not at all.

"What's happening?"

Tim scanned their surroundings. The expression on his face told her everything she needed to know. He didn't have a fucking clue. *What have you done, Tim? Where did you get those stones?*

"It's happening." Tim pointed to the sky directly above them.

Above them the sky was changing.

An orange layer of solid energy grew in the sky. It was in patches like strange clouds. Only, these strange clouds were growing, connecting with one another. Becoming one big cloud. A large part of the bizarre orange energy had already blocked the moonlight, forcing the orange hue to cover everything with its weird tint.

"Tim…" Joana swallowed hard, panic locked on her face.

Tim shook his head, his expression matching hers. "It's the field. It's happening. It's coming down around us. If we don't get out from under this thing before it fully drops down, then we are royally fucked." The palm of his hand pressed against his forehead as he looked up into the growing orange sky.

Joana leaned forward, sure she was about to vomit, stickily from an overabundance of fear. She didn't. Instead something green fell in front of her face dancing right before her eyes. It took a second, but she realized what it was. The odd hue or orange light consuming everything had made the purple streaks in her hair look green. Her skin seemed golden and suddenly she felt like it had changed from night to day. She never was good at shooting skeet like her dad. The weird orange tinted glasses never really did help either. In her opinion, it just made things too bright, which was harder to focus. Maybe she could change her highlights to green. It looked kind of—

"Didn't you just hear what I said?" Tim waved at her. "Fuckin' spacing out on me again… We need to leave!"

"Shhh…" Joana insisted, looking down at the playground. She wasn't sure what was better; Tim yanking her from her cluttered thoughts back into reality, or being okay with the fact that her mind wandered when she was scared. At least then she wouldn't see the end coming. "You want one of those things to hear us up here?"

"I don't give a shit, Joana. We gotta go. Right now! There's no telling how long it's gonna take for the field to drop down, locking us in here with the Arktos'. Don't you get it? If we don't get outta here, we are screwed to high heaven and back."

Joana looked around at the chaos, the filter of orange laid over everything, and she stood up. She smacked her lips and wiped the tears from her swollen eyes. When she wiped her hands on her shirt, she forced the rush of emotions into the pit of her gut. She wanted answers right now. They were in some deep shit and Tim knew it was going to happen too. She just couldn't believe how stupid he could be. How he could let something like this happen. How he *would* let it happen.

"I'm not going anywhere till you tell me one thing." Joana placed a hand on the handle of her machete.

"What…" Tim glared at her as if he needed to give no explanation to any of this.

"Where did you get the stones?" Joana's eyes didn't waver. "Back when we were at old man Terry's house you said you knew that it would work this time. That these stones were different. Where… did… you… get… the … stones?"

Tim started at her for a minute, and then said, "We don't have time for this!"

"Keep your voice down… and again…" Joana shifted her weight from one foot to the other. "I'm not leaving this roof until you tell me."

Tim puckered his lips, and then sucked them in, scowling at Joana. He shook his head from side to side slowly with half-closed eyes. "Fine… alright! I got the damn stones from Miss Yortsdayle! You happy now?"

Joana balked. "Don't tell me you've been hanging out with that old woman. She's bad news."

"Just because everybody in this stupid town thinks she's a witch doesn't make her a bad person."

"Oh my God, Tim. Please tell me you didn't."

"What?"

"Tim, she is a witch. Just look around us. Look at all of this… what the hell were you thinking?"

"What else was I supposed to do. Huh?" Tim shook his head. "Hell, where the crap do you think I got the Geomancy idea from to begin with?"

"I don't know… One of your stupid online games?"

"Wow… really?" Tim rolled his eyes, slapping his hands together hard.

The loud *slap* echoed out across the roof.

Something shifted on the street below them. What followed was unmistakable. The growling hiss of one or more Arktos creatures filled the air at the base of the building. What followed was even more frightening. The rails to the ladder beside Joana shifted; the *clanking* of feet reverberated up it and to the roof.

The koala bears were climbing the ladder.

Joana and Tim were trapped with nowhere else to go.

8

Frank Edelman disregarded everything around him as he slammed on the brakes. The apartment complex's parking lot bustled with activity.

People ran rampant both in and out of their apartments. Some had a chance to escape. Others weren't so lucky as the bear-like creatures gave chase. A body crashed through a window near where he parked, giving him a startle.

Frank took a deep breath and nodded to himself as he clutched the door handle. He prayed he wasn't too late to save Kathie. A quick pull on the handle put him in the middle of the chaos. He sprinted past the creatures feasting on an elderly woman in the grass off to his left. His gaze lingered long enough to realize who it was. A sweet old woman named Mrs. Virgin. No, she hadn't been a virgin all her life, despite the jokes she told regarding the last name. She was the mother of two twin boys, Michael and Gary. They were all grown up now. Frank had only met one of them, Gary. Between the twins, Ms. Virgin was pretty well taken care of. The boys kept her refrigerator full. Made visits to get her scripts filled. Even took her to the hair salon once a month to keep that tight perm round and dyed just right, light blue of all colors. And when one of the first floor apartments had become available, Gary was there to fight for her to get moved from the second floor. It had worked out for her because she loved to be outside morning, day, and night. Frank and Kathie had been there to help her move, which was how they had met one of the twins. Kathie helped by mostly just rummaging through all of her old framed photos of the elderly woman's past life while Gary bitched and bitched about his brother not being there to help. His brother was a jerk, or so Gary had said more than a dozen times. Any time Kathie had come across a good picture she had grabbed Frank and made him look. Some photos were of Ms. Virgin back when she was a teenager. Good looking old lady if you asked him. The payment for helping with the move had been fresh coffee and stories of old. That old lady had some adventures, and Frank and Kathie didn't mind spending the time with her. She was old and lonely.

But now she wasn't moving. That rounded perfect blue hair was now mashed onto the grass while those things fed on her body. She was dead. The creatures' satisfying slurps and grunts confirmed what Frank already knew.

He kept running despite the urge to pull those monsters away from her body.

He ignored all the turmoil. Finding Kathie was his only goal. He disregarded the man standing inside one of the apartments below his at the window looking out with a wide fear filled stare. The eye-shaped beams of light scattered in every direction. The creatures climbed in and out of them like doorways. They carried people dead and alive through the doors.

He didn't question the orange hue that tinted everything around him either. It lit up the night as if it were almost day. It was making his skin seem almost golden and when he took one last look toward Ms. Virgin, her blue hair appeared greenish in color. He even ignored the woman running from her apartment just in front of him screaming bloody murder. Blood covered her from head to toe. He didn't stop. He just darted up the steps to his front door.

He reached the door and jammed the key in the lock.

Swinging the door open wide and slamming it shut behind him, he didn't even realize that there had been no signs of forced entry. He just dashed past the 60" flat screen TV and down the hall, past the framed photos of their last trip to Panama City, Beach Florida for spring break. In the photo, he was wearing a large rounded straw hat and Kathie was wearing an orange two piece bikini. She looked good.

"Kathie... Baby!" His steps were loud as thunder as he charged toward the bedroom door.

She wasn't there. The bedroom was empty. The bed had been made perfectly with more than ten pillows piled on for decoration. He hated those fucking pillows. He slammed the door shut and turned toward the kitchen.

"Kathie... Sweetheart. You okay?" He called out, rounding the corner and locking eyes with it.

He gasped.

It was dead... well, it looked dead at least. There was blood everywhere. On the kitchen floor laid a bear-thing. Its head had been smashed in. A cast iron pot lying beside it was covered in gore. Among the bloody chunks was what resembled *Hamburger Helper* scattered across the floor. He had a hard time wrapping his mind around such a creature after getting a closer look. How could it even be real? It was eerily human.

Frank leaned down to touch it just to make sure it was dead. Its gray fur was coarse and matted in some areas. Blood soaked the hair in some spots, clotted and cold. Its fingernails were thick and black. An image of them slicing at his own face gave him the chills as he felt a cool draft brush across his scalp.

He looked up.

The sliding glass door to the patio was broken. Glass was lying everywhere on the tile floor next to the dinner table. As his eyes scanned the scene, his mind replayed a series of events that he imagined took place.

Kathie had been cooking dinner for them to have when he got home from the Recreation Center. One of those things somehow climbed the patio and broke in. But where were Captain, his dog, and Kathie?

His eyes scanned the bloody beast on the kitchen floor once more and then he careened across the tile toward the broken sliding glass door. There he was, Captain… dead… just lying there under the dinner table. A pool of blood surrounded his unmoving body. His left front leg was missing. Blood trickled across the floor leading to the severed limb.

Franks heart sunk.

"Ca…pt…ain…" He swallowed, his hand over his mouth. "That's my boy," he nodded, forcing back the tears. "You helped protect her, didn't you?"

He turned away, unable to look any longer.

That still didn't answer where Kathie might have gone. The urge to cry came back to the forefront. He'd had Captain since he was a puppy. He shook it off and went to the patio door. Looking out into the strangely orange lit night, the same gruesome scene continued. How he had even managed to make it up the steps and into the house without being seen was beyond him all—

The front door shook with a deafening *boom*. Hissing and grunting echoed out in muffled waves on the other side.

So much for wishful thinking. They actually *had* seen him go upstairs.

Come on, Kathie… where would you have gone?

He glanced back out the patio and saw the tracks. Blood coated the floor on the patio in shoe prints her size. She had made it out. Instantly, his eyes darted to the mushroom key-rack attached to the wall next to the refrigerator. Her keys were gone. A stain of blood left behind where she had snatched them up.

Hope surged through Frank like that fist drag on a cigarette after a few days of going without one. The feeling was there and gone like a flash, the pounding and scratching at the front door bringing him back to his set of crucial circumstances.

He looked toward the living room and the racket that was those things trying to get in, and then back at the patio. He stepped out on it and looked down to the first floor. It was a long way down.

"Fuck. I hate heights."

Someone ran by below and Frank thought he recognized them, but they were gone as fast as they had appeared. If he was going to go for it, now was the time. He checked to make sure his car keys had made it back into his coveralls pocket and climbed up onto the railing.

The sound of a window giving way reached his ears from the living room.

"Motherfucker…" He breathed, climbed down on the other side of the rail. "Just don't look down… just don't look down."

He started to step down from his position, but he had nowhere to go unless he intended just to jump clear to the ground.

There's no way you just jumped, baby. Come on… how did you get down?

He scanned the patio on either side in hopes that it would pop out and bite him like a snake. It did. Bloody hand prints covered the white gutter drain that ran down the side of the apartment. Frank grinned. Just when he eased over, finding his footing to climb down, a creature stepped into his kitchen and locked eyes with him out on the patio.

"Ereht Tuo!" The creature shouted, pointing at Frank.

"Shit."

Frank jumped down clinging to the drain pipe like his life depended on it. Hoping he would slide down like a fire pole, he just let himself free fall, his feet straddling either side of the drainpipe. He slid down faster than expected and landed hard in the bushes below. The wind was jarred from his lungs as he hit the ground. He fell off balance, stumbling over the bushes.

With a jolting *umph* he fell back on his ass. He looked up and locked eyes once again with the creature that had invaded his home from the front door. Only there was more than one up there. It lifted a spear and before Frank gave it the time of day he was up and running away from the now mangled bush that had softened his fall. He heard the loud thump of the spear sticking in the ground at his side. He didn't look back. With the air still not back into his lungs, his chest burned as he raced back toward the GMC. He started feeling lightheaded and dizzy.

He wasn't going to make it.

He needed to stop.

Catch his breath.

But he couldn't. He needed to find Kathie. Get to her before any of those monsters did. If he knew her well, which he did, there was only one place she would have gone.

She would hit Highway 105 and head straight to her parents' house.

The GMC came into view in the parking lot. The orange hue cast over everything made the white vehicle almost too bright to look at.

Frank felt his feet stagger and his ankles buckle. The air still hadn't returned to his lungs. The lights blurred and grew dim. He fell to his knees and pulled the keys from his pocket, reaching out toward the Jimmy as if it would magically place him inside.

"Hey man! Wh...icccchhhh caarrrrr is yourssssss?" Someone shouted.

The words entered Frank's ears as meaningless vibrations.

The dark figure leaned down over him.

"Whhitee..."

Frank passed out, the air finally returning to his lunges a little too late.

The last sound Frank heard as his body fell limp in the grass was the *clinking* of his keys beating him to dirt.

9

When the first murderous other-dimensional creature reached the top of the ladder, something inside of Joana snapped. Fear had caged her in its icy embrace until now. A surge of power swelled from inside giving her mind full control. It no longer escaped to memories of popcorn and sweet treats or any trivial thoughts. She yanked the machete from the sheath, now empowered by the most basic of instincts: Survival.

She lifted the large knife over her head and charged forward unleashing a defiant scream.

It was clear that Tim wasn't going to do a damn thing. So, it was up to her. When those monsters first started climbing the ladder to the roof, Tim had cowered, dropping his weapon at his feet before looking them in the eyes. If he wasn't going to save her, then she had to save herself. She wasn't ready to die. She thought of her parents as she darted across the rooftop howling like a wild animal. Of school and the friends she had made over the years. Of Tim and how things had been when they had first started dating. She longed for that closeness to return. She didn't want it to end like this. Not with things so screwed up between her and Tim.

When she reached the Arktos, fear shot in its eyes. It pulled at her compassionate side. She wanted to reach out, say sorry, and shake hands with it. The bear was just too cute in an odd sort of way. But something took over. Seeing all of the bloodshed thus far in one night had her head flooded in confusion. She realized she had struck the creature square between the eyes when blood splashed across her chest and the blade was coming back down for the second time. The sharp blade slapped wet—penetrating the Arktos in the face with one fierce slice. Blood mixed with matted bear hair sprayed Joana in the chest again.

A sudden, strange humming sound flooded her ears.

When Joana yanked the blade from the dead bear and the creature fell limp from the ladder back to the ground, she realized what the noise was.

Joana stumbled back and fell clumsily to her ass. The blood covered machete still in her hand *clanked* against the loose gravel on the rooftop at her side.

The humming was *her* voice.

Her throat was hoarse, the loud scream still bellowing out against the fact that she was covered in blood.

She had just killed a living creature. It didn't matter if it was going to kill her first. She wasn't a killer. The torrent of thoughts had her mind in knots. She wanted to cry. Tried to cry, but couldn't. The screams rushing from her lungs wouldn't give her tears the room they needed surface.

Another creature appeared at the top of the ladder. It hissed and grunted with fierce intent. Joana's chest felt tight like she couldn't breathe. She had been able to attack once, but she wasn't sure she had any more courage for survival left.

The monster climbed up to the top and jumped onto the roof. Joana froze in fear when the creature locked eyes with her. Drool dripped from its fangs. Its fur covered chest moved in and out with each forceful breath. It pulled a bone knife from its hip and slashed the air while licking its sharp teeth.

Joana tried to back pedal, but couldn't find the will to budge. She tried to call out to Tim. All that fluttered from her lips was a muffled whimper.

The thing stepped toward her.

She gripped at the gravel with her free hand, the rocks crunching between her fingers. Her other hand held tight to the handle of the machete at her side. She wanted to lift it, defend herself. What was the point? She could find the courage over and over again and it would all just end the same. Death. What was the point of living if you had to become something you didn't want to be in order to live? Was it really worth—

The Arktos darted forward.

Joana started to flinch, closing her eyes tight, ready to feel the pain of the creature's blade.

Tim shouted, charging the creature just as Joana had done before.

When Joana looked up, Tim's eyes were wide with rage; the machete in his hand came down hard and fast.

The creature shouted a guttural roar, lifting an arm to block the blow.

One time when Joana was 9 years old, her mother had a piñata strung from the ceiling for her birthday party. It was the kind filled with candy. She loved candy. Always had. She liked Sponge Bob Square Pants almost as much as sweets. The piñata was shaped like Sponge Bob. She loved cartoons and still watched some to this day. She remembered exactly what it was like when one of the boys her age had cheated, not using the blindfold when swinging the bat at the piñata. How the arm just came clean off. The candy spewed out cascading the ground with joyful treats.

This was a lot like that.

Only the Arktos' arm wasn't a piñata. And it wasn't candy and joy spewing from the arm as it separated clean off.

The bear's arm slapped against the gravel at her feet. Blood and sinew sprayed violently from the severed limb. The creature flailed and shouted painful moans. It fell back, dropping the knife from its other hand.

Tim just stood there watching it… watching it suffer. Die.

"Oh my, God. Tim, do something." Joana finally found the nerve to speak up after a minute.

Tim didn't reply.

He remained standing over the bear as it bled to death, the creature afraid. Tim breathed heavily, the machete still in one hand. He almost seemed excited. As if watching this creature suffer was doing something for him. Joana didn't like that one bit. Was he smiling?

Tim brushed his long black hair from his face and stood up straight. "Now that's what I'm fuckin' talkin' about!"

"What the hell are you doing?" Joana breathed, climbing to her feet. "Kill it already. No reason to make it suffer."

The humanoid lay on the gravel leaned against the brick railing. Blood pooled around its body. It looked weak and tired, its eyes shifting constantly.

"My pleasure…" Tim chuckled.

"Oh, God. Don't tell me you're enjoying this." Joana said, looking away from the dying creature.

Tim stepped toward it. It tried to shift, get away, but couldn't. It had already lost too much blood.

"What is that supposed to mean," Tim asked, wiping the machete on his leg then lifting it to the striking position. He grinned and stepped even closer to the creature, taunting it with the tip of the sharp blade.

"Please, Tim… you're going to make me sick." Joana looked away again.

"What's your problem, Joana? It's them or us."

Tim stuck the creature with the machete. Joana closed her eyes. Though she didn't watch, she imagined it all in her mind. The blade piercing the bear's fleshy face. The skull splitting wide open. The chunks of meat and brain seeping out from around the blade. The bear's body going limp and Tim yanking the blade back. The blood flinging in the air as he pulled it free. The sounds it all made began to make her sick.

"Well, it's done. Okay…"

Joana looked up to see Tim wiping his machete on the creature's furry chest. The blood spread across, sticking to the gray hair with ease. Satisfied, he sheathed the blade still looking longingly at his handwork.

Joana wanted to yell at him. Tell him she didn't like the look he had in his eyes. She wanted to be angry at him for it. This was a side of him that she had never seen before. And now she knew, all along, this was the side of Tim she had never met. The side he had refused to let her meet. And for good reason. She wouldn't have dated him to begin with had she known how sick he was. Joanna boiled in disgust.

When she opened her mouth to speak, the exact opposite of all those thoughts came to the surface.

"Thank you for saving me. There's not more of those fucks coming up here, are there?"

As her own words reached her ears, she really had reason to be scared. Scared of what this night would do to her humanity if she made it out alive.

"No… looks clear." Tim nodded.

Joana took one last look at the severed bear arm. The sharp fingernails that would have torn through her like a knife in hot wax had Tim not done what he did. Then that side of her she didn't want to admit existed resurfaced.

"If this orange field thing really is going to come down and lock us in a dome of death then what are we waiting for? Let's fucking do this if we're going to do it," she said, stepping over to the ladder and looking down at the dead bear below. "If we get out of this alive… you owe me big time. This has got to be the worst date you have ever taken me on… ever!"

"I've taken you out on a date before?"

Joana rolled her eyes, sheathing her machete.

"Ladies first," Tim insisted, pointing to the ladder.

"Sometimes it blows my mind I ever dated you to begin with. So, what are we going to do, hit the 105 and just leave?" Joana asked, wondering if Tim even caught that first statement. It didn't look like he had.

"Because if that's the plan, how do you expect us to get there?"

"One thing at a time," he said, waving her to start climbing down. "First, let's just get off this roof. We need to get a set of wheels. That's our best bet."

"I don't know if you noticed, but my mom's car is kind of done for."

"No shit, Sherlock," Tim groaned, grabbing at his ribs again as if bringing up the crash suddenly reminded him to pretend to be in pain.

Joana just shook her head, ignoring him, no longer sure if he really was in pain or not.

When they reached the bottom and found themselves again at the back of the alley, Joana felt like it had been days since they had last been there. There was no telling how much time had actually gone by, what with that strange light casting everything in an orange illumination.

Joana listened for a moment for any activity around them, but heard nothing.

"So, what exactly does this dome of orange light do… *exactly*?" Joana whispered, helping Tim jump down from the last step into the alley.

"To be honest," Tim said, very mater-of-fact. "I have no idea. Miss Yortsdayle wasn't ever clear about it all. I think she left some of the details out on purpose. I just know that if we don't get out in time, we are stuck here with those crazy fuckin' bears until the portals close."

"And how much time do we have?"

"I don't have a clue." Tim shrugged. "But standing here and trying to figure it out is just wasting time, if anything. We need to move."

Not wanting to argue any further how stupid Tim had been for even hanging out with that old lady, blood covered and tense, Joana and Tim eased their way back down the alley toward the street.

Now the real question was whether there was enough time to get out before it was too late. And if Joana was going to be able to cope with the new person she might become at the end of it all.

10

Frank opened his eyes, feeling calm and breathing normally. He was slouched over in the passenger seat of the Jimmy and cruising down the road in a fast clip.

He assumed it to be early morning. An orange hue flooded the sky much like the rising sun. His jumbled thoughts collected slowly. Everything was beginning to make sense.

It had just been a dream. It had all been a bad dream.

The killer bears weren't real. Kathie was fine and driving the vehicle. Captain was probably at the apartment chewing on the sofa. He would tend to misbehave when they left him alone. Especially when taking a longer than normal hiking trip, but he didn't remember planning a hiking trip. Sure, the sky was beautiful, perfect for such and adventure. But he wouldn't have planned something like this unless it was the weekend. And sure as shit not around the same time as that art show at the Recreation Center. He was pretty much guaranteed to get called in at least once on the weekend of those silly openings. There was always something in need of repair.

Perplexed by the situation, he sat up straight and rubbed his eyes. He didn't feel like he had been sleeping in the car very long.

"Were we headed, hon—" Frank started to say. He turned and looked at the driver and jumped in his seat. "Who the fuck are you?"

"Names David Outlaw. Most people just call me Outlaw." The large, gruff man nodded while keeping his eyes on the road. "Gave me a scare there for a second, kid. Glad you came around. Hell, I'm glad I came across you at all. My car is kind of M.I.A., if you want to call it that. No way we would a-gotten out a-there on foot."

Frank stared dumfounded at the driver. He studied the man for a moment. His large forearms were covered in tattoos long faded and blotchy from sun exposure and age. His jeans were grease stained and rolled over his work boots. His shirt was a button-up. It too was covered in grease stains. There was a large tear in the shirt just under his arm revealing some of the man's armpit. The nametag on the shirt read: *Outlaw Tires*. Under that was a name tag: *David Outlaw*. His chin was covered in scruff and a poorly groomed salt and pepper goatee. He wore a worn baseball cap on his head. The John Deer logo embroidered on the front had an oil stain so bad it was almost unreadable.

"Wait… what?" Frank said, scratching at his head.

"Kid, that fall you had must a-been worse than it looked," Outlaw said, looking away from the road for just a second.

"What are you talking about?" Frank looked straight ahead, the road wound left then right. "Are we on 105?"

"The fall… You fell from the second floor of that apartment. I saw it happen. Was a nasty little spill. Hell, knocked the wind right out a-you. For a second there I was thinking you weren't comin' back around. Fuck man, those bears are everywhere."

That was when memories flooded back to the surface for Frank. He wanted to believe it was all a dream. It wasn't a dream. Well, at least if it was a dream, he wasn't awake yet. He continued to stare out the window. The thick trees on either side zipped by in rapid succession. The orange hue that covered everything wasn't the morning sun rising in the sky. No, it was that strangeness that had overtaken the night. He looked at the clock on the dash radio. It was almost 3 o'clock. Still quite a while before the sun was going to decide to rise. His mind replayed from the time he saw Captain dead, falling from the patio of his apartment, and not being able to breathe.

"You pulled me to the car?"

"Yeah, kid," Outlaw said. "Just glad you were able to tell me which car was yours before you passed out on me. Those bears were everywhere. We were lucky we even made it out a there at all if you ask me."

"Well, thanks." Frank smiled. "Name's Frank… people just call me… Frank."

"Don't mention it. Consider us even, Frank."

"How so?"

"Because…" Outlaw shook his head and shifted his hat with one hand. "My truck was ransacked. That's how. Wouldn't a gotten out a-there without you."

"What happened?" Frank asked, checking his pocket for his phone and thinking of trying Kathie's cell again. It was still there. He started to pull it out, but Outlaw spoke up. Not wanting to be rude and cut him off, he just kept the phone in his hand nestled in his coverall pocket.

"I was just drivin' through the area. Headed to 105 like we're doin' now. Got attacked by those things at home. You should-a seen it. They flooded the streets on my block killin' everybody. It was madness. Luckily I was awake and was able to get out when all the commotion started. Again… I was comin' through the area near that apartment complex when a bunch of those *things* just jumped out at me in the road. Hell, I didn't think nothin' of it. I just as much run every one of those sons-a-bitches over. So I didn't try to move. I just kept going right at them. That's when it happened." Outlaw lifted one hand and mimicked throwing a spear. His eyes went wide as he said, "Fuckers took out two of my tires. Lost control and ended up in the ditch."

"Hey, at least you got out of there, yeah?"

"Yeah, no kiddin'," Outlaw chuckled. "Talk about ironic, right?"

"What do you mean?"

"Outlaw, the tire king of Lewisburg just 'bout meets his maker from two blown tires. Shit, I was laughing even when I hit the ditch."

"I guess that is kind of funny."

"Yeah, so that's how we're even. Thanks for the wheels."

"Don't mention it." Frank smiled, pulling the cellphone from his pocket.

"I wouldn't bother trying it." Outlaw shook his head. "I 'bout busted a damn ear drum trying to use mine just before I ran into you."

"What do you mean?" Frank dialed the number, pressing send, and putting the phone to his ear. The instant squealing screech that exploded in his ear from the receiver was so loud that he dropped the phone. The phone fell closed in his lap. "What the fuck was that?" He asked, shoving a pinky into his ringing ear.

"Told you." Outlaw smiled. "Bet it has something to do with what's goin' on. Interference of some kind. Got a-be."

"That's just it… what the hell *is* going on?"

"That's the question of the day, isn't it?" Outlaw said, easing onto the brakes as they hugged a sharp turn on the highway. Once it straightened back out, he gave it more gas. "Some kind government experiment if you ask me. Like the Hunger Games or somethin'. Testin' out some new creatures they done invented. Seein' how they hold up against us armed civilians."

"No way…" Frank scoffed. "And who said anything about being armed?"

"I did." Outlaw leaned over with one hand on the wheel, and used his other hand to pull up his pant leg revealing a revolver. "Never leave home without it. How do you think I made it out of there when I hit the ditch?"

"Makes sense." Frank sighed. "But still… the government wouldn't do something like this, would they?"

"Why the hell not? They do this shit all the time."

"Since when?"

"Okay, well you got a better idea then?"

"I don't know… Aliens maybe."

Outlaw laughed. "Haven't you seen the movies? Aliens don't look like fuckin' bears, kid."

"Whatever… I just don't think the government could pull something like this off. If they were experimenting with cross species genetics or something, I think we would have heard about it."

"You don't have to hear about it. You're seeing it right now, ain't you?"

Frank just shook his head and looked out the passenger window, slightly irritated.

"Look, kid. I ain't tryin' to argue. If it ain't the government, that's fine by me. But I say that's who's behind all this shit until proven otherwise."

"That sounds fair." Frank nodded, looking down at the phone in his lap.

A few moments passed in silence, Frank's eyes never leaving the phone.

"So, who were you trying to call?"

"Kathie… my girlfriend," Frank said, his voice distant. "I don't know where she is. She got attacked at the apartment, but I was too late. I was at work when it happened. When I got to the apartment her car keys were gone and I didn't see her car in the parking lot. She had to of gotten out in time. I just hope she's okay."

"Where would she gone?"

"Same place we're headed. 105 right out of town. Her parents live a few cities over."

"You'll find her. Don't worry 'bout it. If her car wasn't there… she got out."

"Yeah…" Frank said, pocketing the cellphone. "I hope you're right, Outlaw. I hope you're right." Not wanting to think about what could have happened to

Kathie, he changed the subject. "You know… I got my tires replaced at your shop just last month. I always go to Outlaw Tires. Good rates, for sure."

"Yeah?" Outlaw smiled, taking his eyes off the road for a moment to study Frank's face. "I thought I recognized you. We're pretty quick 'bout the turnaround ti—"

"Look out!" Frank pointed to the road ahead, cutting Outlaw off in mid-sentence.

"Oh, shit!" Outlaw shouted, turning the wheel sharp and slamming on the brakes.

The Jimmy shifted hard to the right coming to a stop just in time. The brakes squawked and the axels groaned. The screech of the tires scraping across pavement echoed out through the street even over the groaning vehicle's protest to stop.

"We're never getting out," Frank gasped.

"You don't know that," Outlaw demanded, putting the vehicle in park.

Before them was a five car pileup smack dab in the middle of the highway. Only thing was, there were no cars in the crash coming from the other direction. The cars were just piled on each other like smashed bricks. Orange light floated over the cars like a thick lens. It held them like a cage, preventing them from moving any farther. Three other cars were between the Jimmy and the pile of wreckage. One, a black van, had its back doors open showing it was filled with passengers. Some were obviously injured. More than a dozen more people stood along the street investigating the crash and the strange light coming down like a bowl covering a trapped bug.

Outlaw nodded at Frank and with that, they both opened their doors and stepped out of the Jimmy.

Outlaw called out to the crowd standing near the damaged pileup while walking over. "What's happened?"

No one replied.

Outlaw gave Frank a look and shrugged.

Frank shrugged back.

Approaching the van, Frank saw that there was still someone sitting in the driver seat. An old man. Had to be in his late 60's. Long white hairs protruded strangely from his ears. Frank looked past it and just approached him as if it were any other normal day.

"Excuse me, Sir. Can you tell us what's going on here?" Frank pointed to all the people standing in the street before them and beyond to the pile of cars pressed against the barrier of light.

"So…so…so…something c…c…crazy. That's what," the old man stuttered. "We… de…de…definitely can't get th…th…through."

The old man's eyes darted back and forth, scanning the sides of the street near the woods. As his head bobbed left and right, all Frank could do was stare at those strange hair filled ears. He'd never seen anything like it. Not in real life anyway. It reminded him of that episode of Family Guy where Peter's dad had gnomes living in his ears.

"What are you looking for? Did someone go in the woods?" Outlaw asked, stepping up behind Frank and addressing the old man's wandering eyes.

"Yep... some of the pe...pe...people from the car in front of us went in th...th..there to in...ins...insp...in—"

"Inspect?" Frank filled in the blank.

"Yes..." The old man said, half leaning out the window of the van.

Just when Frank was about to ask why they went into the woods, two people came walking up on the street. The crowd fell silent as they waited eagerly to hear what the two arrivals had to say.

"It's like that all the way down," one of them said, stepping onto the street, slightly out of breath.

"What the hell do you mean it goes all the way down?" Someone else protested.

"That's what I mean, all right? It just keeps going. We can't get past it, whatever the hell it is."

Outlaw stepped forward. "Why can't we just walk through it? It's light."

"You hearing this guy?" A woman shouted. She was wearing a nightgown and slippers. "It's just light... ha... Don't you see these cars, mister? If they ain't passing through, then you can forget about it."

"Yeah," another man spoke up, poking his head out from one of the other cars. "When we first got here, I watched a bird fly right into that damn thing."

"What happened to it?" Outlaw asked.

"It isn't flying anymore if that's what you're asking," the man leaning out of the car said.

Frank looked to the ground and picked up a medium size rock sitting at the edge of the road. Without saying a word, he tossed it as hard as he could at the strange field of light.

"Hey… What the hell are you—" The woman in the slippers started to say, but the collision interrupted her.

The rock collided with the orange field of light with a loud electrical crack. A jolt of pure force and energy pulsed at the center of impact. The ringing *hum* that followed carried through the air like a tuning fork. It was so loud that Frank had to cover his ears. When he looked up, everyone was doing the same.

After a moment the piercing noise faded.

"You think we haven't tried that, mister?" The woman demanded.

"Sorry…" Frank lifted his hands in suggestive surrender.

Frank felt the phone in his pocket burning a figurative hole in his pocket. All he could think about was Kathie. This is the way she would have come. Maybe she made it out before that strange light started filtering into everything. He scanned the wreckage and didn't see her car among the damage. He just longed to call her. To hear her voice. To know that she was all right. That everything was okay. He had to act. Do something. If she wasn't here, then she had to have gotten through. Where else would she have gone?

Just as he was running all of this through his head, trying to think as if he were in her shoes, Outlaw nudged him on the shoulder. They locked eyes and Frank followed him back to the Jimmy away from the crowd in the street.

"Well, what the hell you wantin' to do, kid?" Outlaw whispered, looking back at the mess blocking their path.

"I don't know…" Frank said, glancing back down the road in the direction they had come from. "I'm trying to decide where Kathie would have gone if she didn't make it to her parents. But I just don't know…"

"We could just wait here," Outlaw suggested. "If you really think she would come this way, that is."

"I really do. It's just that she'd be here already. Her car isn't in that pileup… so where does that leave her?"

Frank stood there for a moment just looking around, trying to think of where Kathie would have gone. But more than anything, just hoping that she had made it out to her parents.

"There's another car coming!" The woman in slippers yelled out. "Might want to signal them before they hit us."

"Good point," Outlaw said. "We could a used a bit of a heads up. Came damn close to crashing into this mess ourselves."

When Outlaw and Frank stepped past the Jimmy, someone from behind them yelled out, "It's the police! Thank God. We're saved!"

Sure enough, a cruiser headed down the road at full speed with lights flashing.

For the briefest of moments Frank almost believed it for himself. They really where saved.

Frank swallowed hard, his right hand clasped tight to the cellphone in his coverall's pocket. Maybe in the morning when he woke up in bed next to Kathie they would laugh together about his crazy dream.

He knew better.

The cops in that patrol car were going to be able to handle the situation just as much this was a dream.

They were fucked, and the expression plastered across David Outlaw's face said it all for Frank.

11

"Slow down. There's people in the road!"

"I see them!" Tim grunted, slamming the brakes on the patrol car.

The patrol car skidded across the asphalt coming to a dead stop about twenty feet away from a white GMC Jimmy parked in the center of the road. The cruiser lights still flashed, illuminating everything ahead in purple and green light. The strange orange hue that had descended on the town altered the familiar red and blue flashers.

"What the shit, man? Who parks in the middle of the street like that?"

Joana was too busy lost in thought to have heard Tim's complaint. She couldn't help but remember that white truck. But she just couldn't place it. Where had she seen it before?

Before either one of them could climb out of the cruiser, a mass of people started crowding around. One of them, Joana recognized, which instantly placed where she had seen the white truck. It was Frank Edelman's vehicle. He was a few years older than she was, and he worked at the Recreation Center, but she had seen him around. She had seen him once or twice at a few of the small house parties some of her friends had thrown. She had even talked to him briefly here and there at the grocery store. A jitter of butterflies swarmed in her stomach as he and all the others approached the cop car. He was adorable and handsome all in one.

"What do you think's going on?" Tim asked, appearing hesitant to step out of the car.

"Only one way to find out," Joana said, opening her door.

Tim followed suit and they both stepped out into the street simultaneously.

The calm demeanor of the crowed shifted instantly to an uproar of squabbling and bickering.

"These aren't the police... just a couple of kids!" Someone shouted from within the crowd.

The protests grew even louder.

"What the hell are we going to do now?"

"That's just great!"

"We're all going to die out here!"

"Since when did the police start dressing like Marilyn Manson?"

Frank approached

Joana felt flustered.

"Joana. You guys all right?" Frank put his left hand on her shoulder.

Oh my God... he actually knows my name. What do I do... what do I say?

"I... uh..."

"What the hell happened to the front bumper on this thing?" A large man covered in grease walked up beside Frank.

"Joana, this is Outlaw... Outlaw, Joana..." Frank introduced them. "And the guy with the long black hair... that's..."

She smiled. "That's Tim, my boyfriend."

For some reason or another, she kind of wished she hadn't just blurted out their relationship status like that. If anything, it put her and Frank stuck at just friends automatically.

"Well, nice to meet you guys. Any friend of Frank's is a friend of mine." Outlaw lifted his ball cap, nodded, and put the cap back on. "So I got to ask. What happened to the front end of this here cop car and how in the hell did you end up with it?"

Before either of them could reply, Frank said, "You guys are covered in blood. Are you hurt?"

"It's not my blood," Joana breathed. "Some of what's on Tim is his. He got thrown from my mom's car when those things attacked us."

"Shit, kid. You okay?"

"I think so…" Tim rubbed his head, his face still coated in dried blood. "My head is throbbing something fierce and my freaking side hurts."

"Well, let's get those cruiser lights turned off and you guys come take a look at the damage. Those lights probably aren't helping your head at all," Frank said, looking at Tim. "They're freaking bright as crap."

"We would turn them off, but we don't know how," Joana sighed.

"I got it." Outlaw stepped past Tim leaning into the cruiser. After a moment, the lights went off and he popped his head out with a shotgun in hand. "Check this out. This might come in handy."

"Yeah… We couldn't figure out how to unhook it from the rack either," Joana said.

Tim glared at her with embarrassment. She lowered her head as if what she said was a slap to his face.

"Well, its unhooked now." Outlaw grinned, tossing it to Frank. "You know how to handle this thing?"

Frank caught it and shrugged. "Yeah, I guess. You just point and shoot, right?"

"Something like that." Outlaw smiled. "Just hold tight. It's got a kick to it."

"What about you?"

"Don't worry 'bout me, Frankie-boy." Outlaw shook his right ankle, reminding Frank of the revolver. "I'm covered."

"Hey… what about us?" Tim protested.

"You look like you got it under control if we come into close range assault." Outlaw pointed to the machete on Tim's hip. "Just leave the shooting to us, kid."

Tim rolled his eyes and scanned all of the people standing around them in the street. "Whatever. You said something about a mess up there? What's everybody doing just standing out here?"

"Come take a look."

Frank led them toward the wreck through the crowd with the shotgun resting on his shoulder. Joana watched him walk ahead. He looked so cute in that blue jumpsuit… or coveralls. Whatever you called them. He was a working man. Had a job, unlike Tim. They stepped past some of the people. After Joana smiled at a woman wearing a sleeping gown and slippers, she locked eyes with Tim who had walked up beside her. The look on his face was filled with dread. It was as if he knew what they were about to take a look at. The field thingy that he had mentioned. It had already closed down around them. They were stuck. No getting out. She didn't have to ask. The way his eyes glistened with worry was enough to tell her what she already knew. How could he have been so stupid to let this all happen? Her hatred for him boiled inside. If it wasn't already bad enough, when she reached the wreck, the hatred for Tim grew. The light had kept the cars from getting out.

"Wh…wh…what are we go… go…going to do?" An old man stepped up beside Joana.

"If Tim hadn't—"

Tim jabbed her hard in the rib. Joana winced at the pain.

"What's that?" Frank asked, looking away from the wreckage.

"Nothing…" Tim said, very matter-of-fact. "We just need to—"

A sudden rush of air fluttered beside Tim cutting his words short.

"Run!" Someone shouted.

"Oh my God!" Joana screamed, pointing at the old man that had just stepped up beside them.

The spear protruding from his left eye was covered in blood, the wooden handle stuck out from the back of his head. He slumped to his knees then fell flaccid to his chest on the highway pavement.

Everyone shouted and scattered in all directions. Some jumped back into their vehicles, but once inside were unable to move. The other cars had them boxed in. There was no way to turn around and head back into town. The first Arktos that came into view fell from above. Having jumped from the top of a tree near the edge of the road. It landed on its feet on top of the black van filled with people. It smashed the windshield with a glowing rock. The screams of pain and torment began after it climbed into the van.

"They're everywhere!" Someone shouted, darting into the woods.

"Back to the car!" Outlaw shouted.

When they looked up, the woman in the slippers had jumped into the patrol car. With the keys still in the ignition and the engine running, Joana, Frank, Tim, and Outlaw watched the cruiser take off in reverse. Just as the police car stopped, trying to turn around and take off, three humanoid-bears charged out from the woods on one side, throwing rocks and spears at the moving car. Glass shattered; the bears lunged at it as if it were an animal and not an inanimate metal object. The patrol car stopped and the woman's screamed filled the air for a few seconds. When her screams ended, they knew... she was dead. The car rolled to a stop not even ten feet away from where it had originally been parked.

"What the hell are we doing standing here? Let's get the hell out!" Frank started to run toward the Jimmy, but the three bears that had attacked the patrol car now headed toward them. And the creatures were a hell of a lot closer to the Jimmy than they were.

"Into the woods!" Outlaw insisted, grabbing Frank by the shoulder and pulling him along.

Sharp pain ran through his body as he was pulled down the ditch and past the first few trees. Outlaw had grabbed him right where that spear had hit him. He felt the warm wet sensation of blood running anew under his coveralls.

Arrows came down around them.

"Just keep going!"

Joana screamed, trying to keep up. She could hear the pursuit of those monstrous things giving chase behind her. She stumbled forward almost losing her footing in the soft dirt. She compensated with her other foot and pulled herself forward using a tree for leverage.

She just kept running.

They all did.

With Frank and Outlaw in the lead, Tim and several other people were only a few paces ahead. She looked back, panicked. Those creatures were going to catch up, do things to her. Kill her and eat her.

"Tim! Please… Wait for me!"

Tim didn't even look back. And in moments, she lost sight of everyone else. The deeper she ran into the woods the harder it was to see past all the thick trees. The machete bounced and slapped her hip. The sound of rustling pursuit somehow had changed. It was no longer behind her, but above. She looked up, still running, and thought she saw something gray sliding across the tree line overhead. She heard grunts and that familiar hissing of excitement that the Arktos made. They were surrounded.

Then the trees parted and gave way to a clearing. She fell to her knees nearly out of breath and screamed in terror. Frank pointed the shotgun right at her.

"Duck!"

Just as she did just that, the shotgun fired. The deafening report bellowed out. The creature that had been right on Joana's tail crashed to the ground, its chest blown to bits from the close range gunshot wound. The leaves crunched under its weight as it fell to the ground dead. The glowing stone it held slowly faded, the light leaving it just as the life had left Joana's attacker with the pull of the trigger.

"Thanks…" Joana wheezed, out of breath.

"Don't mention it," Frank said, pointing the shotgun up as he scanned the trees above them.

"How many are there?" A fat man wearing a wife-beater, shorts, and one sock, panted.

"Does it really, fuckin' matter?" Tim said, his machete unsheathed and gripped tightly in both hands. "We're dead."

"Don't say that, kid," Outlaw said, the revolver in his right hand.

All together there were seven of them stuck standing in the clearing waiting for the next thing to happen. There was Tim, Joana, Frank, Outlaw, the fat guy with the one sock, and two other women. One of the women had blonde hair. The other was wearing a tie-dyed t-shirt. Everyone else had either taken off in another direction or was dead. The sound of pain-filled screams echoed out across the woods. From what they could tell it was coming from the road. Frank thought of all those people in that black van and the old man that had the stuttering problem.

"We can't just stand here," the fat man shouted.

"We can't outrun them," Outlaw said, pointing his revolver toward a sudden noise in the woods off to his right. "Our best chance is defense in numbers. We stick together."

"He's right," one of the women said.

"Fuck this… I'm out of here," the woman wearing the tie-dyed shirt said. "I'm leaving before those things realize we're back here."

"That's not a smart move, kid," Outlaw reasoned.

She wasn't listening, and in fact, had already started jogging deeper into the woods.

"Idiot," Outlaw breathed.

"Just let her go," Frank said. "You tried."

Just as those words left his mouth and as soon as the girl was out of sight the screams began. They came from the direction she had just gone. They started out high pitched and terrified. After a moment, they became muffled and gurgle-ish. The screams of death faded and the woods fell silent, but only for a moment. They could hear the bears moving about all around them. Both on the ground and in the trees.

Joana looked to Tim, whose fear filled eyes matched her own. She saw the machete in his hand and followed suit, pulling hers from its sheath. She thought it would make her feel a little better. At least a little safer. It didn't. Not one bit. If anything, it made her more afraid. Afraid that she would have to do things she wasn't prepared to do.

"How many of them do you think there are?" the lady with blonde hair asked, her voice shaking with fear.

"I don't know," Frank said.

"If I had to guess…" Outlaw whispered, scanning the trees and beyond, "At least ten. Yeah, definitely at least ten. And trust me… they know we're out here."

"How do you know that for sure?" the fat man scoffed.

As if to answer his question on cue, a spear flew through the air from the trees above hitting the fat man in the throat. Blood gushed from his neck. He tried to scream, grabbing at the spear jutting from his throat, but couldn't. He just gurgled. Blood bubbled from around the spear's point of entry. The blood pooled around his throat and down his hands to his elbows. It ran down his double chin and plump neck onto his hairy chest, staining the white wife-beater.

The blonde screamed.

With both hands clutching at his throat, the fat man wearing one sock turned and started running in the same direction that tie-dyed had gone. Before he even had the chance to get out of sight, the bear that had thrown the spear fell on him from above. The fat man crashed on his back and the Arktos yanked the spear free. The man gagged against the pain, blood and plasma spraying across the bear. The creature wasted no time striking the fat man in the chest, not once, but countless times. With the spear in both hands, the Arktos enraged, it stabbed the man over and over again. Blood splattered from his chest with each forceful strike.

"Dear God… please help us!" The blonde just started running.

"Shit… what do we do?"

"Back to the car!" Outlaw shouted. I'm taking point. Frank, you cover the rear. You two… just keep up!"

With revolver at the ready, Outlaw took off in full sprint, not even bothering to look back to make sure that the others had followed.

Screams of the blonde that had taken off on her own filled the woods. It seemed painful. Horrid. Agonizing.

"Tim…" Joana cried, grabbing Tim by the hand, determined not to let go.

With Tim in front of her, the machete in his free hand, they ran, doing their best to keep up with their new friend. Joana was afraid to look back. She could hear someone giving chase right behind her. Whether it was one of those crazy alternate universe *things* or Frank was questionable. She didn't want to think about it.

Then all at once, spears and rocks started falling from the sky all around them.

Joana screamed as she felt the wind rushing at her side, hearing the *thudding* sound the spears made as they stuck in the ground around her.

Someone shouted to just keep going. Not to stop.

Outlaw's revolver went off and it sounded like it hit its target. The guttural moan that followed the loud report was somehow satisfying in Joana's ears. The revolver went off again. This time, that satisfying sound didn't follow, no matter how hard she listened for it.

The road was in view.

They were going to make it.

"I think the tire dude got hit!" Tim shouted.

"No… I'm fine, kid," Outlaw demanded, pointing the revolver into the street and pulling the trigger.

Joana watched from over Tim's shoulder as the creature in the street took the bullet and fell to the pavement.

"Come on, we're almost there!" Outlaw jumped out the ditch and back onto the highway.

An Arktos jumped from the trees to his left throwing a glowing rock. He ducked, the rock just missing him. Then he aimed at the creature and pulled the trigger twice. The first shot hit the creature in the chest nearly dead center. The blood exploded at the opening and the bear fell limp to the ground. The second shot *clicked* empty.

"Shit… I'm out!" He coughed, blood spilling from his lips.

When he turned and looked back at the woods, Frank was shoving Joana up the ditch.

"Behind you!" Outlaw shouted, and wiped the blood from his mouth.

Frank spun around, shotgun in hand.

The Arktos that ran on him from behind forced Frank to the ground on his back. He almost dropped the shotgun. The creature pulled a sharp bone-type blade from its loincloth and charged. Frank aimed the shotgun up, pressed the butt of the gun into the dirt for support and pulled the trigger. The gun shook. The loud *boom* reverberated off the surrounding trees. Joana was reminded of the time that Tim put a tomato in the microwave until it exploded. The otherworldly creature's head did just like that tomato. And it looked just like that tomato, too. Red. Red everywhere. The thing's head was just gone. Chunks of muck and blood rained down around it where its head had been.

Joana's stomach churned at the sound the falling pieces of matted meat made as they hit the ground.

"We don't have time to stand around!" Tim shouted, waving his machete. "Whose car are we takin'?"

"The white one," Frank barked, climbing up the ditch.

Grabbing Joana by the hand, Frank ran toward the Jimmy. Watching Outlaw and Joana's boyfriend climbing in upfront, he opened the back passenger door letting Joana in. She turned to him and found herself smiling despite everything. She had never had anyone open the door for her like that. He closed her door and ran around to the other side.

Just before climbing in, more than a dozen creatures filed out of the woods through the ditch to give chase.

"Go… go… go…!" Frank pleaded, jumping into the back seat and slamming the door shut.

A seemingly endless number of spears rained down on the Jimmy. The stone tips colliding with the metal frame sounded like they were driving through a hail storm. Outlaw put it in drive, turned sharply and spun the vehicle around.

As they drove headlong into the path of more than a dozen monsters, the only thing Joana could think about was what happened to that woman wearing the slippers that took off in the police car. She didn't make it out and there weren't nearly as many of them then as now.

"We're not going to make it," Joana breathed.

"Yes we are," Frank said soothingly. He put the shotgun on his lap and reached over, giving her a pat on the hand. "We're gonna make it. I promise."

She leaned into him tight and clenched her eyes shut.

"Hold on tight, kids," Outlaw said, slamming his foot to the floor.

Joana squeezed Frank tighter having felt the vehicle begin to accelerate.

The sound of shattering glass and Tim's sudden scream filled her ears.

They weren't going to make it.

12

The white GMC Jimmy crashed into the torrent of gray fur covered bodies.

The car jolted violently as it pushed through the figures. Bodies rolled over the hood and along both sides, crashing across the cement. The sound of shattering glass Joana had heard had been the front passenger side window. Glass covered Tim's lap. A bear-thing reached in, grabbing a fist full of his long jet-black hair. He flailed and screamed, trying to lift the machete to defend himself. It was impossible to maneuver the large blade into a striking position in the limited space. With the car still moving forward and picking up pace, the creature pulled itself deeper into the vehicle by using Tim's head as leverage. It scratched at his face with its sharp black claws and pulled at his hair trying like hell to gain entrance.

"Fuck me runnin'!" Outlaw coughed, turning the steering wheel sharp right and left.

It worked and the bear fell out of the Jimmy, taking a thick lock of Tim's hair with it.

Tim groaned, holding his scalp and the few cuts on his chin and bottom lip. Bright red blood dripped on his lap. His head throbbed even worse than before.

The back right wheel ran over the creature, lifting the Jimmy for just a moment before dropping back down to catch traction with the road once more.

A new torrent of arrows and rocks rained down from the rear, but before all could reach the Jimmy, Outlaw had spread the distance between them. Only two of the spears thrown in the second wave hit the roof of the Jimmy, bouncing away in the road. The rest had fallen short, the Jimmy clearing their throwing range.

They made it.

"Fuck you, you stupid animals!" Tim shouted, spitting blood onto the side view mirror.

They passed the patrol car on their left. When Joana looked, she wished she hadn't. Two blood covered slippers hung out of the driver side door attached to blood covered legs. That poor woman hadn't made it. As much as she hated it, at least that hadn't been them. She looked over her shoulder and watched the distance between them and the Arktos' grow even wider.

Although not much, the tension lifted.

Frank rejoiced with a *hooting* call. When he lifted the shotgun, bumping it against the roof of the truck, everyone chimed in with him.

"Damn that was close!" Tim smiled, still holding his bloody lip with one hand.

"Thank God" Joana breathed, locking gazes with Frank and giving him a hug.

Tim gave her a stern look, so she pulled away fast, giving Frank an awkward smile instead.

"Talk 'bout…" Outlaw coughed again, pulled a rag from his greasy jeans and covered his mouth. "… a close call."

"You okay, dude?" Tim asked, shooting Joana and Frank a worried look.

"I…" he hacked, stuffing the rag back into his pocket rather fast. "I'm fine. Let's just put some space between us and those fuckin' things."

"Agreed." Frank nodded.

"Tim says they're called Arktos' or something like that," Joana said.

"How would…" Outlaw covered his mouth, "you know something like that?"

Tim sat for a minute and from what Joana could tell he didn't want to talk about it. He didn't want to admit to the blame. Didn't want to be a real man and fess up to the fact that he was the one that brought all of those damn things here to begin with.

Just when Tim looked like he was about to speak up, which surprised the hell out of Joana, Frank spoke first.

"The only thing I can think of is to check the Rec Center."

"For what?" Tim asked, seemingly relieved for the subject change.

Joana didn't intend for him to let it slide. It would come up again.

The Jimmy cruised down the winding road of Highway 105 at a fairly rapid speed. When the curves became too sharp, Outlaw applied ample brakes to compensate before regaining speed. At the rate of speed they were going, they would be back to town within the next 15 minutes. Joana looked over her shoulder again and sighed in relief. Those crazy bear-things were no longer in sight.

"Kathie…" Frank said. "If she isn't at the apartment and didn't make it out of 105 to her parents' house… then all I can think is that she went to my work looking for me. That's the only other place she could have gone."

"Who's Kathie?" Tim asked, clearly eager to force the conversation away from himself. Frank turned to the back, pulling a t-shirt from behind him and handing it to Tim. Tim nodded his appreciation and used it to stop the bleeding on his chin and lower lip. "You wouldn't happen to have some pain killers, too?"

"Kathie's my girlfriend," Frank said, pointing for Tim to check the glove compartment.

Tim dug through it and came away with Advil. Taking several of them dry, he shook the bottle with a thankful nod and put them back.

"Oh… I didn't know you were dating anyone," Joana said.

"Yeah, most people haven't met her," Frank sighed. "She isn't much for going to the parties and stuff like that."

"That's a shame," Joana breathed. "If she's anything like you, I'm sure she's a sweetheart."

"She is…" Frank agreed. "Which is why I need to find her. She means everything to me."

"Awe…" Joana said, looking to Tim with concerned filled, glistening eyes.

Tim just shook his head, shoved a finger in his throat, and pretended to gag.

Joana rolled her eyes at him and turned to Frank. "I'm sure Outlaw wouldn't mind making a stop at your work to look for her before we go to Miss Yortsdayle's house."

"Miss Yortdayle's house? Why the hell would we need to go there?" Frank raised a brow. "That crazy old lady is—"

"Uhh… guys?" Tim interrupted.

Joana scolded him with gritting teeth and disdainful eyes. He just needed to grow up and confess that it was he who opened up all those portals.

"We're slowing down and Outlaw don't look so hot." Tim pointed.

Frank jumped forward in his seat, grabbing Outlaw by the shoulder. The Jimmy was slowing down—fast. The grease covered man lay limp against the driver side door, his eyes closed.

"Outlaw…" Frank shook him.

The truck started to veer hard to the right, Outlaw no longer held the wheel. Tim leaned over the large man taking the wheel as it started to slow to a stop.

"Outlaw!" Frank shook him again, still not getting a response. "David… wake up!"

"What's wrong?" Joana panicked.

"The front of his shirt is covered in blood, man," Tim gasped, only taking his eyes off the road for a moment, still steering from the passenger seat. "I told you I thought I saw him take a hit when we came out of the woods."

"Fuck…" Frank breathed, leaning back in his seat. "Just stop the car."

"I am… I am…" Tim said, keeping the Jimmy centered on the road as it slowed.

Joana hesitated before glancing over her shoulder at the winding road behind them. She just knew that if they stopped, those things would be on them the minute they stepped out of the vehicle.

The Jimmy rolled to a stop. Frank opened his door and stepped out.

"Wait… what are you doing?" Joana said, her tone frightened.

"What does it look like I'm doing?" Frank barked, slamming his door and rounding the Jimmy to the front with the shotgun in hand.

Joana stared at Tim, who stared back still leaning over an unmoving Outlaw. "What the hell happened?" She whispered with wide eyes.

Tim shrugged, returning the facial expression. He reached over Outlaw's body, put it in park and sat back into his seat.

Frank reached the driver's side door, put the shotgun on the roof and pulled the door open. "Come on, Outlaw. What the hell happe… wow!" Outlaw's limp body slumped toward Frank almost falling to the pavement outside the car. Frank grunted when he caught him. "Help me… He's heavy."

Tim just sat there, staring at the lifeless man, Frank trapped under his weight.

"Come on… help me with him."

Tim looked on, shocked.

"Tim…" Joana leaned forward in her seat nudging her boyfriend. "Go!"

Tim seemed to snap out of it and jumped to attention. Climbing out of the car, he ran around to the other side to help Frank ease Outlaw onto the road.

"Here… Set him down there," Frank said, setting him down slowly.

They both stood and looked down at him.

"Is he dead?"

"I don't know," Frank said, leaning down to take a closer look. "What the hell happened?"

"I don't know, man," Tim protested. "He was there one minute, fine… just driving… the next out fuckin' cold."

"You said you saw him get hit when we left the woods?" Frank asked, examining the small tear in the large man's shirt.

He started unbuttoning Outlaw's work shirt. There was a small tear the size of a quarter just above his nametag. The front of it was soaked with blood. Blood that looked like it had seeped its way into the fabric from the inside rather than out.

"Well, yeah." Tim nodded, putting both hands into his jean pockets.

"What hit him?" Frank said, peeling the shirt away from Outlaw's chest. The blood made the fabric stick to the skin, pulling on the large amount of chest hair.

"How the hell should I know? There was shit falling down all around us."

Frank looked up at Tim, aggravated at his lack of sensitivity. But rather than chew him out, the clotted blood on the side of his face, the patch of hair where that bear had taken a big chunk and the swollen lip and cut chin, made him realize Tim had been through enough already. They all had.

"You got that shirt I gave you?" Frank said, calm yet assertive.

"Yeah, but it's pretty much covered in blood."

"Go get it anyway."

Tim nodded and rounded the front of the truck.

"What's happening?" Joana asked Tim just as he poked his head in to get the bloody shirt.

"I don't know, but it doesn't look like he's breathing. I think he got hit when we were leaving the woods and he didn't say anything."

"We got to do something…"

"Can't you see we're doing it?" Tim lifted the shirt that he had used on his lip and left Joana sitting in the back seat.

Joana leaned up to get a better look, but was unable to see anything from her vantage point. Paranoid, she looked over her shoulder once more at the winding road behind them. This was just no good. Couldn't they just have Tim drive and let Frank look Outlaw over while the car was still in motion? Those things were still out there back at the wreckage. And with nowhere else to go, surely they would be working their way down the highway back toward town. Just thinking about it, her stomach tightened and she felt something climbing her throat to the surface. Hell, if the man wasn't breathing, then just leaving him and moving on would be fine by her. She thought about that again and realized the cruelty behind it. She was no better than Tim. The excitement he got from killing the bear on the roof. She was no different. Maybe they were actually made for each other. Tim was right. It's us or them. And the same was true for Outlaw. It was us or him.

That same feeling rose in her throat again just thinking about how much this night was changing her. Her nerves were working against her.

Joana opened her car door, stepped out, and vomited. The warm wet cascade of bile splashed across the pavement at her feet.

She groaned, wiping her mouth, and looking back the way they had come. Still no bears in sight.

With her stomach temporarily relieved, she stepped around her open door and took a look at Outlaw. He was lying on the pavement, leaning against the side of the Jimmy. His skin was pale and his shirt unbuttoned and pulled back. His chest was covered in blood and hair. More blood than hair, at that. A quarter sized hole just above his right pectoral muscle seeped crimson. The blood flowed freely.

"What happened?" Joana asked, smacking her mouth against the foul taste of vomit.

"Something got him, but I don't know what," Frank said, leaning over the body. Both of his hands were covered in crimson like he'd been sticking his fingers in a red paint bucket. "I tried to dig it out, but whatever it is, it's in there pretty deep."

"Did it go through the other side?"

"Good question…" Frank said, nodding at Joana. "Let's have a look see. Here, Tim… help me flip him over."

While Tim and Frank rolled the large man over, Joana found herself staring down the road in both directions. This wasn't good at all. They were wasting time. And if anything, they were like sitting ducks just camping out in the middle of the road. This was not the place to be. She could just feel it.

"What the fuck is that?" Tim gasped.

"I don't know…" Frank said.

When Joana looked back down at Outlaw's unmoving body, she saw it. Whatever it was, it went straight through his chest and all the way to the back just below the skin on the other side of his body. It was round and glowing. The blue pulsing circle made Joana think of that sling the bear had thrown in the park to catch that woman. Then she thought of the stone the bear dropped right after Frank had shot it with the shotgun. That had to be what it was. But even still, how the hell could one of those creatures throw one of those stones so freaking hard, and so freaking fast, that it would dig that deep into Outlaw's chest like that?

"It's a stone," Joana breathed, not even realizing she had spoken out loud.

"Yeah, I think you're right," Frank said, looking at Joana and then turning to Tim. "Let me see your knife."

"Please don't tell me you're going to do what I think you are?" Joana swallowed hard, watching Tim hand over his machete.

"He's already dead," Frank said, taking the blade and using the sharp end to dig the glowing stone free.

"We don't have time for this," Joana said, looking over her shoulder.

Frank groaned. "Got it..." he said, the bloody stone popping free from Outlaw's back.

It fell from Frank's hand and skittered across the pavement at his feet. Just as it came to rest next to him they all watched as the glow that had once been there faded away, making the stone just become an average looking rock.

"Here... let me see that," Joana said, picking it. She wiped the blood off it with her shirt and studied it. The shape, the size, the weight. It was the same.

Her mind's eye flung her through the past back to old man Terry's backyard. It all seemed so long ago. All those stones she was holding in her shirt while Tim through them at random through the yard. They were just like this one. "These are just like the stones you got from Miss Yortsdayle, Tim."

Tim glanced at the rock for a second. "I don't know what you're talking about."

"Bullshit, Tim. You know exactly what I'm talking about," Joana scoffed, done playing games. "This rock is just like the stones you got from that stupid witch. The ones you used to open up all those portals and let those fucking bears loose... you know, *those stones*."

Frank stood up, the machete still in his hand. "Do... what?"

Tim took two large steps back.

"Tim got some magic stones from that crazy old lady and used them to open all those portals. He even knew about the field dropping down around us. There's no way to get out either."

"What the fuck!" Frank leaped forward, snagging Tim by the shirt collar before he could get away. He slammed him into the side of the Jimmy. His long dark hair danced in front of his skinny pale face. Frank lifted the machete and shouted, "Give me one good fucking reason why I shouldn't cut you up right here, you little shit."

"Please... no..."

"Shut it!" Frank glared at Joana, and then turned his attention back to Tim. Still pinned against the Jimmy, Frank shoved him hard again and brought the machete to his face. "So let me get this straight!

My friend Outlaw here is dead… because of you. Kathie has gone missing and could be any fucking where, because of you. My fucking dog! My dog, Captain is dead, because of you!"

"Look, man," Tim protested, trying to squirm free. It was no use.

Joana thought to plead for Tim's life, but didn't know what to say. Frank was going to go through with it. She just knew it. It was in his eyes. That maddening look. Maybe Tim deserved it. All of this was his fault. Hell, maybe it was just as much her fault, too. Maybe she should take the blame. Maybe then Frank would take her out of her misery. Then she could die in peace knowing that the situation hadn't totally changed her, made her entirely heartless. If she was going to die, she wanted to die with at least a little heart left.

"Please, no…" Joana said softly. "He knows what's happened. Between him and Miss Yortsdayle, we have a chance… Please!"

Frank glared at her hard and long, his eyes never wavering from that mad look of pure carnal hatred. Joana felt her heart race, beating against her chest even faster with the growing tension. Frank's grip on Tim tightened and he slammed the scrawny gothic kid against the car again.

"Please…" Joana's voice was soft.

Frank shook his head with disapproval, raised the machete at Tim, and yelled as the blade came down fast.

13

The sharp blade slammed down hard. The loud metallic *clank* echoed across the highway pavement, the machete crashed down hard on the Jimmy's hood right next to Tim.

Joana screamed while clutching her eyes shut tight.

"What the fuck, yo?" The voice wavered with a hint of distress.

It was Tim's voice. He was alive.

Joana opened her eyes, her heart still racing. Frank loosened his grip on Tim, but not after shoving him hard once more into the side of the truck. The machete was still in Frank's hand. A large dent in the Jimmy's hood next to Tim left scrapes of white paint on the center of the large blade. Frank flung the machete to the ground glaring at both Tim and Joana. The metal blade *clinked* and *pinged* against the asphalt, coming to rest in a puddle of blood next to Outlaw's corpse. The quarter sized hole in the gruff man's chest had seeped out a tremendous amount of blood in the short time they had been on the street. It pooled around his shirtless body, the work shirt tossed to the side a few feet from the Jimmy.

Joana gripped the small stone in her hand, squeezing it hard as the silence built awkwardly around them.

Frank finally tore his eyes away from the two Goths, and gazed at the tattered and bloody work shirt peeled from Outlaw's carcass. Breathing a heavy sigh and running his fingers through his hair, he unzipped his coveralls just low enough to reach into his jean pockets. He grabbed his cigarettes and lit one up before stuffing the pack back into his pants. He puffed on the cigarette a few times, exhaling a plume of smoke over his head and then zipped his coveralls back up. He stepped away from the Jimmy and turned his back to Tim and Joana.

"Look… I…" Tim started to say, but Joana locked eyes with him and shook her head.

"Just give him a minute," she whispered.

Frank stood there in silence, not once looking back at his two new friends. With each tender drag of the cigarette he seemed to calm down. It was clear; he was thinking about something.

When he was finally done, he turned back around, dropped the butt to the cement and stepped on it.

"I just think we—"

Frank shook his head, cutting Joana off. "I don't know what's going on or why or how. And frankly, I don't want to know, okay?" His words were calm and assertive. Putting both palms in the air facing Tim and Joana, he said "Look… As much as I want to say I over reacted, I didn't, and I sure as shit ain't sorry. If you really do have something to do with all this crap, all I can say is…" He pointed a finger at Tim, his voice still calm. "You got what's coming to you. Trust me."

"What the hell is that supposed to mean?" Tim barked.

"Don't even push me, punk." Frank stepped forward. "From what I can tell, you've given me good enough reason to kill you right here… right now. You got that?"

His eyes didn't waver. He just stared Tim down. Tim swallowed hard and nodded, still leaning against the truck.

"I…" Joana started to say.

"I wasn't talking to you," Frank hissed. "Now, I said… do… you… got… that?"

Tim nodded.

"Good…" Frank leaned over Tim making the Gothic teen shiver with fear. He grabbed the shotgun from the hood off the Jimmy and pointed it at the boy. "You're probably wondering why I'm even keeping you alive. Hell, I'm asking myself that same damn question."

Frank shook his head, tossed the shotgun back into the Jimmy and started to climb into the driver's seat.

"Why?" Tim asked, his voice wavering.

"Because…" Frank said, slamming the driver's side door shut and rolling down the window. "You know something I don't. And on our way back into town, you're going to tell me everything you know. Now get in."

"But what about the body?" Joana said, looking down at Outlaw's corpse still leaning against the Jimmy.

"What about it?"

"We can't just leave it here like this. It just isn't right."

"Hey… don't get me wrong," Frank said, sticking his head out the window. "The guy was nice and all, but I didn't know the man. Did you?"

"No, but we can't just leave him here. Those bears will do things to his remains. What if this was you?"

"Joana…" Frank said, pointing out of the truck at the body. "That isn't me. And if it were… do you think I would really give a shit? I'd be dead. Now let's go. Both of you… get in."

Joana sighed. She wasn't the only one being hardened by the events of the night. She hadn't known Frank very well, but she had gotten a sense of who he was. And a heartless killer with no compassion definitely wasn't something she thought she would have ever seen in him. She just shook her head and rounded the truck with Tim to get in. Funny thing was, she didn't really care either. She just knew that in the movies they always took the time to bury their dead regardless of the circumstances.

I guess real life just isn't the movies.

She climbed into the back seat with Tim, afraid of the future.

Frank put the Jimmy in gear and took off down the road, once more headed back toward town. Joana looked back and watched as the truck created distance between them and the tire repairman's unmoving body. It was sad. What was sad wasn't that it was happening. No, what was sad was that even in the middle of it all, she *wasn't* sad. Just like that woman with the slippers in the cop car; at least it wasn't her.

"So start talking, Tim," Frank said from up front, his voice stern.

Tim reached over, taking Joana into his arms and sighed.

That was when he confessed.

He told Frank everything. How he was related to Miss Yortsdayle. And that everyone's assumptions about her were partially true. She wasn't a witch, but she did know quite a bit about the dark arts and about spiritual things in general. He told him about the sack of stones that she had given him and how they would open up the portal to another world. He pleaded, swearing up and down that he didn't mean any harm to anyone and that doing the Geomancy ritual had just been his hope of leaving this world for a better one. Frank wasn't having any of that, so he went back to the details. The details of how he knew about the possible existence of the Arktos creatures. There were many stories about other worldly creatures. There were worlds beyond worlds out there. Other dimensions. He admitted that although his aunt told him about the Arktos, he didn't believe that humanoid bears could exist.

"Yeah, just like portals to another realm don't exist, right?" Frank scoffed, rolling his eyes at the Gothic teen through the rearview mirror.

"Look, man," Tim cried, holding Joana tight. "You wanted me to tell you about it… I'm telling you about it."

"That's all well and good, but can we send them back?" Joana asked.

"I don't know," Tim said. "My aunt says they will leave when the portals close."

"And when is that?" Frank grunted.

"I don't know that either."

"Well, what the hell do you know then?" Frank gritted his teeth, keeping his eyes on the winding road.

"I know that we need to go to her house. If anyone can tell us how to stop this thing and give us some answers… it's my aunt."

"Fuck that!" Frank chuckled.

The truck fell silent, Frank's high school tassel swinging from side to side under the rearview mirror.

"Well, you got a better idea?" Joana asked.

"Yes, I do! We're headed to my work. If Kathie went anywhere, it would be there."

14

The parking lot of the recreation center bustled with chaotic activity. Things were becoming stranger than they had already been before.

"Hold the line!"

"What the hell's happening, Captain?"

"Do I look like I know, Officer?" Captain Grimes shouted, squeezing the trigger of his 9mm for what seemed like the hundredth time. "Just keep firing!"

The Rec Center parking lot was a warzone.

More than twenty cars formed a line on one side of the lot to the other creating a single barricade of both police and civilian vehicles. With their backs to the large recreation center building as a protection from the rear, the firing line did what they could to keep the strange otherworldly attackers at bay.

In the midst of the chaos and panic, Captain Grimes had managed to pull together more than half of the small town's police force along with a hefty chunk of the armed citizens of Lewisburg. If you asked him how he had managed such a daunting task in the midst of such turmoil, he wouldn't have been able to tell you. In truth, a lot of it was sheer luck. He had managed to corral what civilians and police that were out in the streets doing the same thing he found himself doing after being abruptly awakened by the bear-like intruders; fighting for survival. None of the radios worked. His cellphone was shot and no one knew exactly what the hell was going on. That was another thing not quite explainable. He wasn't sure if he would live through the night. If he did make it to see another day, there was no way in hell anyone would believe him. Killer koala bears from another dimension wasn't an everyday occurrence. While he stood pulling the trigger, reloading, and pulling the trigger again, he had a hard time convincing himself it was true. He was just thankful to know that the right to bear arms was still in effect. Because it was that right to bear that was helping them even fight these… these fucking bears. He chuckled at that and pulled the trigger again.

"I'm out!" The officer beside him shouted, ducking behind a patrol car. His eyes were like Captain Grimes had seen countless times. Fear filled. His lip quivered as he dug through the duffle bag on the ground between them for another clip. "We're going to die…"

"Don't say that, officer," Grimes said, firing a shot and then ducking down behind the same patrol car, but not before seeing one of those bear-things take the bullet in the chest. He smiled. "Here… let me see if I can find what you need."

He came away with a fresh clip for the young officer beside him, and then snuck a peek at the chaos on the other side of the car. Guns of almost every make and model reverberated around him with an endless cacophony of fire. It had been going on like this for more than an hour now and there was no telling how much longer they would be able to stand. Ammunition would run out sooner or later. By the looks of it, sooner would come quicker than later. He looked up and down both sides of the barricade of cars. Men wearing camouflage wielded long range hunting rifles. Others wore the same thing as the captain—practically nothing but an undershirt and boxer shorts. Among the twenty-car barricade, there had to be at least forty men, all doing their best to keep those beasts at bay.

On the other side of the firing line things looked much different. A torrent of arrows and strange glowing rocks rained down around them. The trick was to keep those crazy bears far enough out that their aerial attacks couldn't reach the safe zone. So far, for the most part, the surge of fire power had managed to do that. But that was about all it was doing. For every single bear that fell, two more seemed to take its place. The street was full of those things.

When the young officer beside him finally got the clip reloaded, and leaned up to start firing again, Captain Grimes glanced over the patrol car and pulled the trigger.

Fuckin' death trap, he thought, leaning back down behind the cruiser.

From the looks of it, the street just beyond the recreation center parking lot was overrun with those creatures. He wasn't good with numbers, but just from a quick glance, he had to guess there were at least five of them for every one behind the barricade. Something had to give, and soon.

"Where the hell are they all comin' from?" A large man named Taiter with a graying big beard grumbled. He lifted his hunting rifle, peering into the scope and he pulled the trigger.

Grimes followed the gun's line of sight and watched the large man's deadly accuracy. The bear took the bullet right between the eyes. Blood spurted at the center of his head, the back gushed an explosive spread of brain and grey matter.

"No idea… Taiter." Captain Grimes said, squeezing off two shots before ducking down. He and Taiter, along with several of the other men in the line had gone hunting together countless times. As much as having a familiar face at his side, this was somehow much different than shooting at deer and hogs. "What the hell you think's goin' on?"

"Your guess is as good as mine, old man," Taiter said, dispensing the shell from his rifle and reloading. He shook his head, his big graying bear rattling his chin. "I don't know much, but looks like they're comin' from those lights at the far end."

Grimes stole a glance at where Taiter pointed. Sure enough, there were a few strange beams of light and those bears were climbing in and out of it like it was some kind of doorway.

"I don't—" Taiter started to say.

The young officer on Grimes' other side shrieked. When Grimes and Taiter looked, it was too late for the young officer. One of the bears had gotten close enough, throwing an arrow right over the barricade. The young officer fell limp to the ground beside the duffle bag of ammunition, the small spear sticking out of his left eye. Blood ran down his cheek.

"Shit…" Grimes breathed.

"I'm totally out," another officer said, crawling up beside Grimes and Taiter. "Oh well… they got Pete."

"Yeah…" Grimes grimaced, looking down at the arrow sticking out of the young officer's face.

"Here… take this." He reached down, taking Pete's gun and handing it to him.

"Thanks," the officer said, taking the 9mm.

Grimes nodded, shoving the officer to move down the line and keep firing.

He acknowledged and moved on.

Grimes and Taiter watched the officer move three cars down before stopping, taking aim, and unloading the 9mm on those things.

Taiter raised the rifle again, took aim with the scope and pulled the trigger. The report didn't even seem that loud. With all the other guns going off around Grimes, it was drowned out by all the others. His ears rang and although he didn't see the animal take the bullet, Grimes knew Taiter had hit his target. The smile plastered on his face suggested yet again another precise hit. He smiled back at the big man, then aimed and fired off a few rounds himself. The pistol stung in his hand with each pull of the trigger. His bones were getting too old for this. Each time he pulled the trigger, pain ran down his arms to his arthritic elbows and up his shoulders to his boney back. He gritted his teeth against the pain with every shot, just happy to know that there was one less of those *things* left to face.

Suddenly, the hail of spears and rocks stopped.

The bears shouted with excitement all in one accord.

When Grimes looked over at Taiter, what he saw was something he never expected. Taiter was a big strong man. Never afraid of anything. The time they had all been out hunting and he had nearly severed one of his fingers. Not a single tear. The only time

Grimes had ever seen the large man even crack, just a little, was the day Taiter's baby girl had been born. But even then, his expression was cold stoned, unless you knew Taiter and knew what you were looking for. When Grimes stared up at him now, fear clung to the old police officer's gut like wet noodles to a wall. Taiter's face was gripped with terror as he looked out at what was happening with those animals in the street. Whatever it was, those creatures were getting excited.

"I don't want to look, do I?" Grimes cringed.

Taiter didn't even reply, his gazed locked on whatever was going on out beyond the parking lot.

The chills that ran up Grimes' spine forced him to look. It was then that he realized the entire firing line had stopped shooting. Everyone was transfixed by the unrealism and horror.

"Oh… God…" Grimes gasped, using his thumb to rub an imaginary crucifix across his forehead, down his chest, and along his shoulders.

The crazy bears chanted with arms raised in the air. And by all means they had damn good reason to be excited. Initially, some of the portals behind the mob of attackers had been blocked from Grimes' and the other's view. With the bears' numbers growing, what was going on behind them had been hard to see, but now that was another thing entirely. Somehow or another, those things had managed to make one of the blue pulsing portals of light grow and it was growing even now. Before, the portals had only been just big enough for the humanoid bears to climb in and out. Now the one right behind the mob of excited creatures was nearly six times the size and getting larger. The pulsing blue hues of white and baby blue stretched out across the orange sky.

Then... then it happened.

Something unimaginable started climbing through. From the looks of it, it was having a bit of trouble; the portal too small.

"What... the hell is... that?" Taiter breathed.

"I don't think I want to know," Captain Grimes said, checking the clip in his 9mm.

The massive creature was nearly half way through the beam of light, its long snout and big ears just breaking through into their world.

"Is that a fuckin' elephant?" Someone shouted several cars down the left side of the barricade.

That is exactly what it was. It was an elephant. Only it wasn't just any normal elephant. The animal looked three times the size of any that Grimes' had seen on television or at the zoo. Maybe it was the fact that it was walking on its back two legs like a human. Just like the upright bears, the elephant was wearing primitive clothing. One thing that Grimes noticed was the thick rope tied around its ankles, arms and neck. As the creature stepped through the portal, he could see that the rope was still attached to something on the other side. Like a mammoth beast, it had monstrously large tusks. The massive creature fully penetrated the portal, stepping into the street. Its long gray leathery trunk reared back, its mouth open. A large guttural roar bellowed out across the parking lot like a triumphant trumpet. This excited the humanoid bears even more. They shouted with excitement and raised their weapons. Then Grimes realized why the rope was there. This elephant was a captive beast. The bears were controlling it. Three more humanoid bears riding on the backs of large red kangaroos penetrated the portal, stepping into the street behind the elephant. Each bear riding a kangaroo held the back end of the rope, keeping the elephant confined to his restraints.

"This is not happening," Taiter gasped, locking eyes with Grimes.

"I've been saying that since I got out of bed," Grimes said, slamming the clip back into place. The satisfying *click* assured it drove home. "Unleash hell on these bastards! Fire at will!"

Captain Grimes was the first to fire off a shot. That was all it took. The entire barrier of cars unloaded all at once with a hail of torrential fire power. Grimes' ears rang, but he ignored it just like he ignored the arthritis.

One of the bears riding the kangaroo took a shot in the face. Grimes knowing it hadn't been him that made the shot, watched the creature fall off his mount, blood exploding from his nose. As much as that was exciting to see, the elephant flailed. Only having two bears holding him back rather than three, the large mammoth beast tore free from its restraints and charged. Its loud guttural roar resonated like a brutal war siren. The first few charging steps it took had been on just its back legs. Once it was off the street and in the parking lot headed for the barrier of cars it dropped to all fours picking up speed.

The elephant collided with the patrol car Grimes had been huddled behind. Having seen it coming, Grimes jumped from his perch in Taiter's direction.

Had the explosive collision not been so loud, as the elephant's tusks tore into the cruiser sending it back several feet, Grimes might have heard his bones protest against the fall as he fell in Taiter's lap.

Screams echoed out, followed by the sound of smashing steel. When Grimes looked up, the elephant was stomping the cars down the line. It charged forward with its sharp tusks impaling the officer that Grimes had given the gun to only moments before. He took the hit dead center of the chest. The mammoth creature reared back, the young officer still stuck to the creature's left tusk, the massive bone protruding out the officer's backside.

The torrent of arrows started to fall again, this time much closer than they had been before. The bears were advancing. Spears started colliding with the cars and getting closer.

"What do we do?" Taiter asked, trying frantically to reload his long-rifle.

When Grimes looked up to lock eyes with his friend and fellow hunting mate, he was startled by a loud *thud* just above his head.

A massive red kangaroo pounced on the hood of Taiter's truck, hissing at Grimes. The bear riding its back growled something almost human. Grimes didn't even see the spear leave the creature's hand. One thing was certain. He sure as hell felt it. The sharp stabbing pain surged through his chest and back as he fell to the cement. He reached up feeling the wooden handle protruding from his chest. That was when he heard the screams and torment all around him. It was coming from both sides of the firing line. The blood ran warm and free. He coughed crimson, looking up at his attacker. The last thing the Captain saw before he died was two koala bears attacking Taiter. One yanked at the long graying beard, stabbing the large man repeatedly in the abdomen. The other sliced his throat, and from what Grimes could tell, the bear was smiling when it happened.

15

"Talk about B-freakin' movie!"

"What?" Frank whispered, peering around the building's edge at the madness happening in the Recreation Center parking lot.

"Yeah, attack of the Outback. You never saw that one?" Tim said, leaning over Frank's shoulder to get a better look.

"No…"

Having neared the Recreation Center by only a block and a half, Joana urged Frank to stop the car in the middle of the street while they were still out of view of the parking lot. She even made him turn the Jimmy's engine off; swearing up and down that she could hear something. Reluctant, Frank was ready to get there, greet Kathie with open arms and go, but he did as she asked and found himself thankful that he had complied. They all were. The noise was faint, but there nonetheless.

Screams.

Guns firing occasionally.

The noise seemed to ricochet off the buildings around them as they sat in the middle of the street a little over one block over.

They didn't sit there long. When Frank started the Jimmy again and put it into drive, Joana reached up, grabbing his shoulder. He flinched, the joint still sore from his spear wound.

"Ouch! Be careful. I've got an injury"

"Sorry. I didn't know. We shouldn't just head into the middle of something. What if there are a lot of those *things*?" Joana said.

"Good idea," Tim agreed.

Frank shrugged.

The three left the Jimmy and slowly jogged to the cover of some trees on the side of the street. Frank had the shotgun. In truth, he had no idea how many bullets were left in it—if any. Tim and Joana still sported the bloodied machetes on their hips. Tim's showed a hint of white paint peeking out from under the sheath. They walked the entire block in silence. Had there been any shadows to stay under to conceal them as they hugged the buildings they would have used them. There were no shadows anywhere. The strange orange hue of light that sealed the city in an impenetrable dome of energy pushed the darkness back. All of it. Before the Recreation Center reached their view, many other unspeakable things did. Mangled bodies and unrecognizable body parts lined the streets. There were a pile of at least three blood soaked bodies smeared across the sidewalk. Frank led them across the street to avoid getting close to the stench that permeated the air. Flies already had taken claim to the meaty loose morsels left behind by the killer bears. Crossing the street to avoid it hadn't helped and they in fact walked right up on a severed head. It was upright on the sidewalk, eyes openly staring directly at them. Frank nearly stepped on it before jumping back just before his foot came in contact. The strange thing was that although the skull was crushed, pink meat and pus seeping from the opening, the man's glasses were still on his face, only the left lens cracked slightly. But that wasn't even the most eerie thing they saw. They passed a pulsing blue portal. It was shaped like an eyeball, yet vertical. What was scary about it were the markings on the street. There were blood and dirt streaks like what you would see if you dragged a body through a pile of mud covered razorblades. The streaks were going to the portal of light and ended right under it. Whatever, or whoever, had been dragged right there was pulled to the other side. Dead or alive, none of them wanted to think about it. They all looked in silence and just kept on walking, not once making eye contact during the whole thing.

Joana protested the entire idea, just wanting to go back to the truck. Frank urged them on, insisting that Kathie needed him. That was when they reached the edge of the building they were at now, peering out from its corner at the Recreation Center parking lot.

It was a blood bath from the pits of hell and back—times three.

"Well, you're seein' it now, dude!" Tim insisted, replying to Frank's having not seen the movie.

"How the hell are we going to get in there?"

"Easy. We ain't. And that's that." Tim nodded. "And if you got a problem with it, then feel free to step up and stroll on over there by yourself. Cause I sure as shit ain't headin' out there. What do you take me for? A moron?"

"Look. You started this. You're stepping out there and helping me go find her."

"Bullshit. You want to go out there and commit suicide, be my guest. But I ain't going. No way… no how."

Frank fell silent while they all looked on.

There had to be more than a dozen different cars lined up in a row in the parking lot. The entire place was a mess. There were bodies everywhere scattered across the parking lot and flung all over the tops of the line of cars. There were even guns scattered about. Everything was red. It covered the place like a thick blanket your grandmother might have sewn for you when her hands weren't quite so cramped. More than fifty upright-walking killer koala bears were either standing together in the parking lot or just looking around. Others scavenged the area, picking at the loose bones and bodies scattered everywhere. Then Joana gasped, pointing. She didn't even have to say it, because they had all seen it at the same time. There were three other creatures walking around among them as tall as a two story house. Mammoth elephants. That's what they had to be. Their ears were spread wide, the long tusks and narrow trunks unmistakable. Just like the Arktos creatures, the elephants wore clothing and walked upright. One of the large leathery beasts even had what looked like a body still hanging from one of its tusks. The police uniform was a dead giveaway as the body lay limp still attached the large protruding bone. As the mammoth beast walked about scavenging the area of mangled remains, the dangling uniformed corpse pivoted and swayed with the elephant's steps.

Gun shots rang out far off in the distance to the right of the Recreation Center parking lot. Frank and his two Gothic friends followed the sudden cacophony of firepower. They were surprised to see a band of survivors rounding the side of the building toward the back. Several Arktos' gave chase following with spears and glowing rocks in hand.

"Oh no…" Joana gasped.

"Nothing we can do about it," Tim said, looking away.

"As long as they keep going, they have a chance," Frank said, looking on. "From what I could see there were at least four of them. And only three of those bears were after them. Since they were well armed, they got a fighting chance."

"Yeah, as long as none of the other ones decides to catch them off guard around the other side of the building," Tim laughed.

"But…" Joana shoved him, disgusted.

"What?" He shrugged, still smiling.

"Nothing…" she grimaced. "Can we just get going now? I don't like this. Being out here like this. This far away from the car. What if we get spotted or something? We need to turn back. There's just way too many over there to handle." She looked up, pointing toward the parking lot massacre. "And those elephant things… I don't even want to think what would happen if one of those things—"

"Shh…" Frank cut her off, kneeling lower against the wall.

"What is it?" Joana gasped.

"Be quiet," Frank urged, lifting his hand. He lowered his voice, his eyes wide. "A few of those things in the parking lot are looking in this direction."

"Shit…" Joana heaved. "Please… can we go back to the car? I would feel a lot better if we—"

"What part of shut the fuck up don't you get?" Tim said, leaning over Frank to see what was happening in the Recreation Center parking lot.

As if getting slapped across the face, Joana reared back, stunned. Tim had never talked to her like that. Just when she was about to bark back at him, Frank spoke up.

"Shit… We've been spotted!"

"Move!" Tim shouted, turning to run back toward the Jimmy.

Joana screamed, catching a quick glimpse of more than ten bear-men charging in their direction. That wasn't what made her scream. The elephants were charging along right behind them. The ground shook with a furious trembling as the stampede surged forward. She felt her shirt yank hard, nearly choking her. When she looked up, her legs kicking into gear on their own, Tim had her by the shirt running at full sprint back the way they had come. She felt the rolls in her thick midsection bouncing up and down as she ran. Not even six feet from the side of the building they had been huddled behind, her left side started to burn, the muscles not used to the work. Out of breath already as she heaved with every step to keep up, she watched Frank and Tim ahead of her. Their rampant pace was one of fright. And when she saw the expression plastered across Frank's face that single second that he decided to look back, Joana knew. She swallowed hard forcing herself not to look back. She felt the animals giving chase. And the feeling was more than enough sensation. She didn't need to see it, too.

With each foot plunging forward, one before the other, over and over again, the pain in Joana's side surged unbearably. When her vision began to blur, the lines fading together into one large abstraction of color, she wasn't sure if it was the pain in her side or the grip of fear causing it. Her chest felt hot, her throat dry and restrictive.

They were almost there.

The Jimmy was in sight.

She was so gripped with panic she didn't even realize that she had already run the block and a half that they had walked. She had run right past the severed head of the man still wearing the glasses. Past the portal of horror, the stains of anguish sliding right up to the eerie light leading to another world. Right past the scattered body parts and blood that stained the streets.

"Get in!" Someone shouted.

Joana wasn't sure if it was Tim or Frank. She was too busy losing her nerve to pay attention.

The back passenger side door swung open and she lunged forward, jumping in. She instantly felt relief set it. As if the vehicle was a security blanket that protected her from monsters, she took a deep breath of release. For the briefest of moments she was back home, age 7, tucked under her covers and totally okay with the fact that the closet door was wide open.

She was saved.

"Oh shit!" Frank screamed, the Jimmy roaring to life as he jammed the shifter into gear.

Joana looked up.

The horde of creatures fell on them the street. Just about every last one of the beasts that had been rummaging through the parking lot of mangled bodies must have left their hunt for new, fresh meat. The road was a cluster-fuck of upright walking animal attackers. Shoulder to shoulder they charged forward, not even fifty feet from the white Jimmy. A hail of arrows left the mob ascending into the air above them. Somehow it reminded Joana of those times when she and Tim would nestle up together real tight on the couch watching scary movies and making out. Of all the movies to come to mind right then, the movie *300* flooded to the surface of her scattering thoughts. Something about the arrows blotting out the sun. Only there was no sun. Only orange.

The Jimmy kicked into gear, peeling out in reverse. The tires squealed as they caught traction. The sudden jarring motion sent Joana plummeting from the back seat. Her head hit the seat in front of her as she collided with the center console between the two front seats. The truck spun, someone shouting '*shit, shit, shit, shit, shit…*' She tried to sit up but the rapid motion of the vehicle made it hard to gain control, her eyes only finding the back of Tim's head and the ceiling.

After a few moments, the car seemed to settle, still surging forward. Joana pulled herself up and turned herself around sitting in her seat. Frank was at the wheel, his knuckles pasty white as he gripped the steering wheel intent on keeping the truck from crashing. Tim looked back at her, but not at her. He was looking through her, his eyes wide and his mouth agape. She followed his gaze and looked over her shoulder. The mob had fallen behind by a quarter mile, the vehicle too fast for the creatures on foot.

She sighed, her heart pounding in her throat.

"All right…" Frank exhaled, Joana watching the tension lift from his shoulders just a little. "This aunt of yours… what gives?"

"What do you mean?" Tim asked.

"I mean, what gives? What the hell is she going to do to fix this crap?"

"I don't kno—"

"She can fix it, I just know it," Joana cried, cutting Tim short.

"I never said that."

"Whatever!" Frank hissed. "If she can help us, that's all that matters!"

"Yeah…" Joana sighed, feeling the tears build. "How do we get to her house, Tim?"

Before Tim could open his mouth, Frank said, "I got it. I know how to get there." His voice was hard, his grip still tight on the wheel. His eyes never left the road. "Just know that if we get there and she can't help, you two are fucked!"

The air in the Jimmy turned silent for a few minutes as the truck rolled down the street at a rapid pace.

"What the hell is that supposed to mean?" Joana stared at him in the rearview mirror.

Frank locked eyes with hers for a second. What she saw in him was almost demonic. His eyes were so wide that the whites showed unnatural amounts and his unyielding scowl never wavered. Rather than reply, he reached past his coveralls, pulled out his pack of cigarettes, and lit one up.

The mood the rest of the ride to Miss Yortsdayle's house was grim.

Engrossed with fear, the silence ate into Joana like termites in old wood.

16

The Jimmy rolled to a stop only two houses down from Tim's aunt's house. The road had been eerily silent during the drive. Although the hue of orange light made everything seem as if it were day, there was something about the street that was very different than any of the others they had driven down on the way there. With his window down, Frank leaned half out looking around.

"Strange…"

He didn't have to explain the statement to the others.

They knew exactly what he meant.

The homes on this small, practically vacant street were undisturbed. Other than Miss Yortsdayle's house, there were three others on this small dead end road. There were no mangled bodies lying in the street. No blood splattered across the pavement. No primitive weapons left behind, or remnants of a massacre. No portals of light floated in the distance, suggesting the alien visitors might decide to drop in unannounced.

It was still and… well, strange.

It was as if the people that lived on this dead end street were still snuggled in their beds unaware of any mayhem and chaos flooding the streets in other areas of town.

The house to their left was just like the others. The lawn was unkempt, the grass and foliage growing out of control. The mailbox was wrapped with what looked like poison ivy. The thin brick walkway that led through the tall grass from the mail box to the front door was practically nonexistent under the high grass. None of the lights was on in the house, and from what Frank could tell, the house had been vacant for quite some time.

In fact, that was how all of the houses appeared.

Even Miss Yortsdayle's.

The grass and vines that poured out from the ground up engulfed her yard and home like a strangling set of tentacles trying to choke out any ounce of life left on the property. The one thing that made Miss Yortsdayle's house stand out from the others was the walkway. It actually looked to be mowed down, not by a lawnmower, but by trampled feet. And Frank knew exactly why that was. She was one to keep frequent visitors. He had been in her house once or twice with Kathie. Kathie was into all of that mystical crap. The sign in Miss Yortsdayle's yard right next to the trampled path was also covered in a choking stronghold of overgrown vines and grass. Although parts of the sign were covered it was still readable. In an almost Celtic font, the faded and peeling paint sign read: *Psychic Readings of the Supernatural Kind*. The letters at one time must have been a dark red against the painted white wooden sign. Now the white was cracking and almost absent. The once red lettering was now a pink washed out fade of what it once was.

"Do you think those creatures are still headed this way?"

"No telling," Frank said, looking at Joana in the review mirror at the back of her head. She was looking back the way they had come. "But if they are, I'm sure it will be a while before they catch up to us. They were on foot and the witch's house is like eighteen miles from the Recreation Center."

"She ain't no witch for the last time," Tim argued. "She's just... different. Lots of people go to her for help. And there's nothing wrong with that. She's more like a doctor. It's just that her medicine isn't average."

"Yeah, right," Frank chuckled, flicking the ashes from his cigarette out the window. He brought it to his lips, inhaled and spoke while still holding his breath. "More like a witch doctor."

Joana snickered at that and Frank blew the plume of smoke from his nostrils while smiling at Joana in the rearview mirror.

"Whatever, man," Tim cringed.

Frank sat there a moment longer enjoying his second cigarette with the window down. He felt uneasy about the situation. Something was off. Not only was the street silent and void of activity, it seemed like the closer they got to Miss Yortsdayle's house, the more it got that way along the drive. It was almost like all of the crazy Arktos things, as Tim had called them, had gathered at his work to form one massive mob. With that, there was hardly any activity anywhere else. He didn't like that. If they were met with a few, he knew they had a chance. But how many of them were back there in the parking lot was just way too much. And he wasn't one to believe in luck, like his girlfriend Kathie. They might have gotten lucky once, getting out of there alive back at the Recreation Center, but there was no way in hell they'd make it out of something like that twice. There was just no way. It didn't matter how the odds looked. That many creatures coming down on them like that wasn't something he wanted to face again. And looking on at Miss Yortsdayle's house sitting here on this dead end block was unnerving. If those things did decide to descend on them here at the old witch's house they were fucked. No way out but the way they came in. With that, he knew one thing to be true. If those bears did take the time to make that long walk all the way here, they would be coming down on Frank and his friends the same way. He didn't like the idea of being blocked in on three sides with only one patch of road leading the way out. It was a deathtrap. He exhaled a long exaggerated breath of smoke. The smoke almost seemed translucent as it rose against the orange strange light that engulfed his vision in all directions. Its unnatural appearance gave him the shivers. He tried remembering the line of cars back at the Rec Center parking lot. Was one of them Kathie's ca—

"So are we going in there or what?" Tim asked, pointing at the old rickety house.

"Fuck it," Frank said, tossing the cigarette out the window and opening his door. "Let's do this."

When he stepped out, slamming the door shut, he heard the two other doors on the other side do the same. Joana and Tim rounded the front of the white Jimmy and looked to Frank as if he were supposed to lead the way.

"I don't think so." Frank nodded at Tim, nudging toward the house with his nose. "Your aunt, your lead."

Tim's shoulders sagged, a grunt of protest hinting in his inflection as he sighed.

Frank just shook his head and Tim got the hint.

Leading them up the unkempt lawn, Tim directed the way. The grass that hadn't been trampled along the path by Miss Yortsdayle's various visiting customers folded under their steps. A twig snapped just as they passed the mail box. Joana jumped, a faint whimper fluttering from her quivering lips.

"It's all right," Frank encouraged, softly pushing Joana along while looking over his shoulder at the Jimmy.

Joana looked down, taking Frank by the hand. He nodded at her, letting her take hold and he helped lead her up the porch steps to the front door.

When they reached the top, Tim stood at the door and hesitated. He froze in place looking blankly at the door handle.

Frank scanned the porch, Joana still holding his hand tightly. To his left was an old wooden porch swing. One of the chains had broken long ago. The swing leaned half on the ground and half in the air suspended by the one working chain. To his right on the other side of the door there were a plethora of candles, all shapes, sizes and colors. All of them had been used to some degree. They lined the porch railing, both on the floor and on the railing itself. They were hanging on the windowsill. A single wooden table laid in the corner of the porch covered in candles, the wax dripped down all along the sides—long hardened.

Tim knocked on the door.

Tap… Tap… Tap…

Frank felt Joana's grip tighten on his hand. He squeezed back.

A light flickered on from inside. The abrupt flash made Joana gasp. When Frank looked over at her, she looked as if she was holding her breath.

"Hey…" he said, soothingly. He ran his fingers through her soft, dyed hair. "There's nothing to worry about, okay? Tim's aunt is going to help us. Remember?"

"Yeah…" Joana lowered her head, obviously trying to make herself believe that.

Frank caught an ugly look from Tim. At first, he wasn't sure what it was for, but then he realized. Tim didn't like him being all touchy-feely with his girlfriend. He smiled at Tim, releasing his grip from Joana's hand. Sadly, if Tim wasn't going to comfort her, someone had to. Since Kathie wasn't there for him to take care of, he felt like it was his job to take care of someone. Tim sure as hell wasn't doing it.

The soft pitter-patter of approaching feet reached the front door from the inside.

The curtain on the window to the left of the door peeled back revealing Miss Yortsdayle's pale face. She smiled, left the window, and opened the door.

"Come in… come in…" She said waving them in, her voice frail and brittle like thin glass. "I've been expecting you all."

The little old lady at the door was at least in her early 80's. It had been several months since Frank's last visit with Kathie. In truth, he thought all of this hocus-pocus crap was just one big joke. She short and slightly hunched over. Sopping wet the little old lady probably didn't even weigh 100 lbs.

She was thin, a bag of bones. The clothing on her body sagged. The shirt she wore had a bunch of strange symbols on it that Frank had only seen when visiting her little place of business. But to call your home where you sell incense and trinkets a business wasn't something Frank could really call a home. More of a waste of time. Her shorts were the same dark red as her shirt with none of the odd round and square symbols on it. The shorts were short enough to reveal her boney kneecaps and thin liver spotted chicken legs. She was barefooted. Favoring her right side, her right hand held an old wood cane made from what looked like the branch of a corkscrew willow. The wood had a dark stained shiny finish.

She waved them in.

Tim entered first, followed by Joana, and then Frank.

She smiled up at each of them as they came in. Her smile was wide; the false teeth overbearingly out of place in her narrow head. Her skin sagged and the liver spots that covered her from head to toe only made the perfect pearly-whites in her mouth clash against the look of old age.

When she turned to close the door, she said "Oh, one more thing before we get a pot of tea started."

Frank looked back at her as she stepped to the door.

She reached into her shirt at the collar pulling free a small purple stone attached to a thin rope around her neck. She lifted the stone and chanted three little words with her brittle little voice.

"Degos… bynata… seagintada…"

Frank, Tim, and Joana watched as the stone in the little woman's hand started to glow. She smiled and waved it back and forth over her head. As this happened, they all watched as the orange hue that had fallen down around them was pushed back. Night fell upon them once more. The darkness consumed Miss Yortsdayle's yard as it crept in like a fog.

When she was done, she placed the stone back into her shirt, letting it dangle around her neck out of sight.

The darkness had pushed back the light barrier only up to the street. The front end of Frank's Jimmy was sticking in just at the barrier's edge. Part of the truck looked normal. The rest of it was still cast in the orange hue, making the white paint bright and hard to look at.

"How the hell did you—"

"It will buy us some time, yes? Keep them out, no?"

"How did you do that?" Frank asked.

"It's all in the stones. The stones hold the key young boy. Don't you know this already? Haven't you seen its power tonight? Oh, yes… yes…" She smiled, closing the front door and escorting her guests down the narrow hall toward the living room. "I'm sure you have seen many wonders tonight."

"But…" Frank said, pointing over his shoulder toward the front yard.

"Yes… to answer your concerns, young boy. They are coming. We haven't much time. No, not much at all. The field will keep them at bay for a spell. But how long… that is the question. Isn't it?

Now come… come. Into the living room. You've come seeking answers. This I know." She laughed, pushing Frank forward down the hall. "I know many things, come to think of it."

"And Kathie?" Frank breathed, locking eyes with the frail old woman.

"In time, young boy, in time. Now let's get ourselves comfortable in the kitchen. These old bones can't handle standing for very long. They need their rest, but first how's about some tea?"

A loud hiss of hot air from the kitchen came just as Frank and the others reached the living. It startled Frank.

The tea was ready.

17

When Frank and the others entered the living room, it was exactly as he had remembered. Everything in its place and a place for everything.

The living room walls were lined with old torn and cracking wallpaper that must have been there since the house had been built, back in god-knows-when. By the looks of the striped green and brown wallpaper, Frank estimated the house was at least 80 to 110 years old. The stone fireplace was covered in dust and probably hadn't been used in years. A huge framed portrait of a middle-aged couple hung above the mantel. On his last visit to the shop with Kathie, old Miss Yortsdayle had told them both an elaborate story about how the photo was of her great grandparents and that it had traveled overseas on a pirate ship or something. It truth, like many of the things the old hag had said during the stupid visits, he hadn't much paid attention to the story.

The curtains lining the windows, which overlooked the front yard, were the same as the fireplace. Dust covered. The entire house was just a fire hazard waiting to happen. The lights were down low, only one small lamp in the far corner barely doing much to drive the darkness back.

Really, the living room was less of a living room and more of a shop. Shelves lined the walls on all sides, excluding near the windows. The shelves were about chest high and housed a variety of books. *Candle magic. Find your Center. The Inner Light. The Chakra in us All. Soul Food.*

All of it nonsense.

Other than the shelves of books, Frank knew he could care less about, the room was stacked with Wiccan paraphernalia. Candleholders, incense burners, pentacles, and all kinds of other silly crap were stacked on different tables. Each piece individually priced for sale.

A lamp sat on a display case at the far end of the large living room. An old dusty cash register rested on top. Small impulse purchase trinkets were displayed in little wooden bowls, but the real treasures were the stones and crystal shards arranged on shelves. Some of them seemed to glow against what little light reflected off them from the small lamp. The others didn't stand out as much. They just didn't have that same shine, which was probably why they were priced lower. Frank snickered to himself. He still just couldn't get over how all of this was just a bunch of horse shit. This was a waste of time. He needed to be out looking for Kathie, not in here goofing off.

And just as that thought flashed in his mind another took its place. That thing she did with the necklace on the porch—pushing the orange light-field back and causing it to be night time again just around her house. Talk about some crazy shit.

And with that… now things were different and he intended to be all-ears, no matter how outlandish and stupid the old lady started to sound.

He followed Joana, Tim, and Miss Yortsdayle past the storefront area into another room. Rather than a door to open and close, the doorway was lined with beads that Frank had to push aside as he entered. The beads *rattled* in his ear like a hissing snake. The room was one he had been in a time or two before with Kathie. The fortune telling room. One large round table sat in the center.

The room was as cliché as it could get. Mirrors along the wall. The glass ball on the table. This old chick had it figured out. He couldn't blame her. Gimmick sales. And gimmicks she definitely had plenty of.

As they passed through the fortune telling room into another area that he had never been before, the *hissing* whistle of the boiling pot of water got louder and louder with each step.

The kitchen was surprisingly bright, unlike the rest of the poorly lit house; the overhead lights in the kitchen were all on. The tile floor was a bright white and the counters and cabinets painted a baby blue. The entire room reminded Frank of something out of the 1950's. Steam shot out from the kettle's spout whistling its hatred for pressure. When the little old lady reached up removing it from the stove's burner, the steam settled and the noise faded.

Miss Yortsdayle looked ages older in the harsh light, the liver spots covering her skin much more apparent. She set the cane against the counter, waddling over to a small door next to the stove. It was odd. The door had two handles on it. One on the left and one on the right. She reached over grabbing the left handle. When she opened it, the shelves on the other side of the door were lined with dishes. She reached in, retrieving five mugs. When she looked back at her visitors, she sighed, putting one of the mugs back in its place. She set the four mugs on the counter and closed the door. She then reached over and grabbed the handle on the opposite side. When the door swung open in the opposite direction, Frank's jaw nearly dropped to the floor. The shelves were no longer lined with dishes. Instead they were filled with spices and cooking seasonings. She pulled a clear jar down that was filled with sugar cubes and closed the door.

"How the hell did you do that?" Frank gasped.

"She can do crazier stuff than that, trust me," Tim said, looking down at Frank and Joana's joined hands.

"I take it one of you didn't make it," Miss Yortsdayle said, obviously ignoring the comment about her pantry.

"Yeah, but how would she know that?" Joana whispered, still holding Frank's hand.

Tim stepped over, scowling at Frank and Joana. He took her by the other hand, yanking her away from Frank. "You need to back up, man."

Frank just rolled his eyes at the young immature punk and turned his attention to Miss Yortsdayle. "Excuse me, miss… how did you know that…"

His words trailed off, Joana unable to hear him because of Tim. Her boyfriend pulled her aside at the far end of the kitchen and locked eyes with her.

Keeping his voice low enough for just the two of them to hear, he said, "What the hell gives, Joana? You got the hots for this guy or something? He's a fuckin' janitor, for Christ's sake."

"What are you talking about?" Joana said, trying to still hear Frank and Miss Yortsdayle's conversation. The old lady, from what she *could* hear, was talking about David Outlaw and how he was supposed to be with them. "I just—"

"Just nothing, Joana." Tim grabbed her by the arm, still keeping his voice low. "What am I supposed to do?"

"I just need you to be here, Tim," Joana pleaded.

"What the hell does that mean? I am here. I freakin' helped get us here, didn't I?"

"Well, yeah…" Joana sighed. "You are here. But you're not *actually* here."

"What the hell is it with women being all cryptic and shit?" Tim shook his head.

Joana started to explain, but it looked like Frank was getting frustrated with Tim's aunt. She walked over, handing her and Tim warm mugs of tea.

"Here you go, sweetie." Miss Yortsdayle smiled, the mug shaking from side to side in her unsteady hand.

"Joana took the mug and returned the smile. "So, aren't you a little old to be Tim's aunt?"

"Oh, yes… yes…" She nodded, turning back toward the stove and shuffling over awkwardly without the use of her cane. "I am actually in no way related to Timothy. I was, however, there when he was born. Watched him grow from afar, yes. Me and his mother were close… once. Not now. Times change, no doubt."

"So you're not actually related?"

"Nope," Tim said, lifting his steaming mug to his cut lips. "Still, I've known her all my life. Look up to her like a second mother, I guess."

"Come… let's have a seat," Miss Yortsdayle insisted, waving them to the small table pressed against the wall in the corner. There were three chairs. She took one, Joana and Tim took the others while Frank stood. "I remember it like it was yesterday. I was there when Timothy was born. What an event." Her eyes glistened and her smile went wide as if rehashing the events in her mind. "He wasn't born in the hospital like most babies these days. No, back then Timothy's mother was a different woman. Free spirited. A natural birth was the only way to go. And the only way I would ever recommend—"

"No offense…" Frank interrupted. "I don't think that now is the time to reminisce, do you?"

Miss Yortsdayle's smile faded along with that glistening look in her eye.

"We don't mean to be rude," Joana butted in. "But we were hoping you could help us."

"Yes… the stones." The old lady nodded. "Of course… of course."

"We want to send them back," Tim said. "How do we do that?"

"You mean the Arktos ?" Miss Yortsdayle sipped from her mug. "The best way to have done that would have been to never bring them here."

"Well, that wasn't exactly planned." Tim cringed, looking away from his friends.

"Of course not, Timothy. Of course not. You didn't intend on any of this to happen when you came asking me all about the Geomancy rituals. Had I known you were going to steal the stones from me, I would have never told you how they worked. The multi-verse isn't something you can just toy around with, dear."

"You stole them from her?" Joana hissed.

"The multi-what… the geo-what… What the hell are these stones?" Frank looked flustered.

"That's how this all started," Joana said, looking up at him. "You know this. We went over some of it in the truck. The stones… you know."

"Yeah, but I don't see how a handful of stones could do something like this. Something like what I saw her do with that one around her neck." Frank pointed at Miss Yortsdayle. "And what the hell is the multi-whatever."

"The multi-verse," Tim breathed, taking a sip of his tea.

"That's right," Miss Yortsdayle said, looking up at Frank. "You have heard of a parallel universe, no? It is one and the same."

Frank nodded.

"Well…" Miss Yortsdayle continued, "The multiverse, or meta-universe, is more than just a hypothetical set of multiple possible universes that together comprise everything that exists and can exist. It's more than that, because it *is… that*, you see? Yes… the entirety of space, time, matter, and energy as well as the physical laws and constants that describe them are all comprised of the multi-verse. Worlds within worlds that are in turn within worlds. The possibilities are endless. Humans on one world. Talking bears on another. Whatever your mind can fathom is a possibility."

"So those bears out there are from another universe?"

"Something like that." Tim nodded.

"And the stones? I just don't see how that could ever work? Magic stones… come on."

"Oh no, my boy. They are more than just magic. Magic is just a force. The stones are much more than that. They all are. Stones have power over our names. Over all things."

Miss Yortsdayle stood from her chair. The wooden legs *screeched* against the tile as she pushed it back. She eased herself away from the table and made her way over to the stove. Frank, Joana and Tim watched as she set her mug on the counter and proceeded to pour herself another cup of tea.

Frank leaned over within earshot of Tim, and said, "Dude, your aunt is nice and all, but I don't see how going over all of this shit is getting us anywhere. We need a freaking game plan. Not only for how to get rid of those fucks, but for in case they decide to show up at her front porch."

"Hey…" Tim whispered, throwing both hands in the air. "You're the one that keeps asking her questions. Not me. And the whole multi-verse is kind of her soapbox, so… I don't know what to tell you there."

"Do you really think they're going to show up on the porch?" Joana asked, her eyes wide with concern.

Before Frank could answer her, Miss Yortsdayle eased her way back to the table.

"Now, where was I? Oh, yes… yes… of course. Of course," she said with that old and fragile voice. "The stones."

"Miss…" Frank started to interrupt, but she didn't pay him any mind and kept on with what she was going to say.

"Have you ever read the Bible? Well, I guess it doesn't matter. The stones. They're in there too. Even Jesus of Nazareth talks about them. And who was Jesus?"

Joana raised her hand as if in grade school.

"Yes, dear?"

"He was Christ, right?"

"True. Very true indeed, but not the answer I was looking for." Miss Yortsdayle smiled, watching Joana lower her hand. "He was and is the corner *stone*. Do you see? Do you see?"

Miss Yortsdayle's excitement increased while she sat there letting it sink in for her visitors.

The three stared at her blankly.

"Oh, me, oh my. Yes… yes," the old woman said, starting to get back up. "Where are my manners? Who else wants some more tea?"

"I would," Tim said.

Frank stepped forward, not letting the old woman stand, while waving at Tim and shaking his head no. "We're fine, really. Please… we are thankful for the hospitality. But we need to get to the meat of the situation. A mob of monstrous creatures from another world. The multi-whatever. I'd like to get around to the part where you tell us how to send them back to wherever the hell they came from."

"Of course… of course." Miss Yortsdayle nodded, sinking back into her seat at the table. "The stones. Yes… I was getting to that."

"Good." Frank bowed, stepping back a little to give the woman some personal space back.

"He who has an ear, let him hear what the Spirit says. To him who overcomes I will give some of the hidden manna to eat. And I will give him a white stone, and on the stone a new name written which no one knows except him who receives it."

"And what does that mean?" Joana asked, setting her empty mug down on the table looking into it emphatically.

"Well, it means…" Miss Yortsdayle continued, "stones have power. This we know. But how do they have that power? Christ Jesus, son of God, was made the corner stone by his father. With him as the first living stone, an omnipotent force, the rules were changed. If you possess the stone, you have access to worlds beyond this one. *He is* a foundation. The foundation on what all facets of reality are built on."

"The afterlife," Tim chimed in.

"Yes… yes." Miss Yortsdayle smiled. "For those who have made it, taking possession of the stone that transports them to the new realm he has given them new stones. Imagine thousands of stones, one given to each of us who make it to the new realm, or Heaven. Holding individual powers all their own. A name that is only known by the beholder. You see… do you see? There is power in the names. Names hold power."

Frank stepped away from the table, walking over to the kitchen sink and looked out the window. The darkness in Miss Yortsdayle's backyard was still there, the stone she had used still keeping the field of energy at bay by a few hundred feet. Beyond her backyard he could see the orange hue or light eager to surge forward consuming them again. Letting those creatures in. He thought of the highway and how those cars were piled up, unable to move past the field. He knelt forward, looking up through the window at the sky. It felt good to see the stars overhead. He sighed, still trying just to wrap his mind around it all.

"So, how the hell do stones and names have anything to do with the situation now?" Frank turned around leaning against the sink.

"Like I said before…" Miss Yortsdayle stood from her chair and waved at the two kids to help themselves to more tea. Making her way to the pot of warm water, she said, "Imagine that there are many stones with many different uses and powers. Somewhere down the line, stones were lost, stolen, or worse… taken by force."

"And the stone around your neck?" Joana asked, walking up behind the old woman and pouring herself a fresh cup of tea.

Miss Yortsdayle patted the stone hidden under her shirt and smiled. "All things come with a price, I suppose."

"Hell, that reminds me." Tim snickered. "How you pushed back the field like that. What is that orange field all about anyway?"

"The Arktos have stones of their own. Yes… yes they do. It was not them that penetrated our world. It was us that imposed upon them. The field is a safety they have set into place. Keeps them from being out numbered during the extermination."

"Extermination?" Joana gasped.

"Well, yes," Miss Yortsdayle said, turning to make her way back to the table, her mug filled to the brim. "The portals will close when they leave. And they will leave when there are none of us left. The Arktos aren't the only ones who have ever been invaded. There are many others. Sad... sad business it is, if you ask me."

"Sad? What the fuck are you talking about?" Frank demanded. We aren't the ones slaughtering them by the hundreds."

"True." Miss Yortsdayle sipped her tea. "But we *are the ones* whose government have known about these stones for quite some time and have used them to enter other worlds more times than I can count. Where do you think our rapid technology comes from? Other worlds. What do you think Stonehenge is? A portal. The stones are the key. We don't know where or why it was built, but that is because the government wants to keep it hidden."

"Bullshit." Frank rolled his eyes.

"Fine. Don't believe me," Miss Yortsdayle hissed. "I don't care. Nope... no I don't. Not one bit. I don't need to tell you how to stop them anyway. It's just all make believe. Frank, you think I don't know how you feel about all of this? Kathie is smart to trust in me. To trust in what I know. Because what I know *is the truth*!"

Both Tim and Joana looked on, stunned and wide eyed. They had never thought of hearing such a harsh tone from such a little old woman.

"And furthermore," she continued, staring up at Frank with beady eyes, "we are running out of time.

The Arktos and their minions will soon be at my porch. We need to act… and fast—"

Frank's cellphone rang out loud, both vibrating like crazy in his pocket and cutting Miss Yortsdayle short.

When he reached past his coveralls and yanked the phone from his pocket, his heart raced. His palms began to sweat and his knees began to buckle. The magic trick that the old lady had done, pushing back the orange field, must have given him signal reception once again.

It was Kathie!

"Hello? Kathie? Baby…"

18

Frank paced the kitchen floor, the phone glued to his ear. The smile plastered across his rosy cheeks told Joana that Frank was happy. It made her feel good to know that his girlfriend was okay. She hadn't heard anything coming from her end of the conversation, but from the way Frank was acting it was all good news.

Joana breathed a sigh of eager relief. Seeing Frank like that reminded her of humanity and nearly losing hers in her fight for survival. She was going to make it and she sure as hell was going to maintain moral values in the processes. She sat there watching him pace back and forth smiling from ear to ear between every word he spoke.

"Why don't you take a picture?" Tim rolled his eye, resting his chin on his fist, his elbow planted on the kitchen table. "It'll last longer."

"Oh, come on, Tim… really?" Joana said. "Jealous much?"

"Well, yeah. What of it? You've been ogling him since we ran into him on the highway. Don't pretend like I'm wrong. I've been watching you. And it hurts my feelings."

Joana looked to Miss Yortsdayle, who sat across from her and observed all of them, then back to Tim. "You suddenly want to talk about feelings?" She rolled her eyes. "That's all I have ever wanted was for you to pay attention to my feelings. You never do. And don't deny it. You know I'm right. And that's that."

"What are you talking about? Don't turn this around on me. You're the one holding that dude's hand."

"You always do that, Tim. Once you get shoved in a corner, you try to turn it around." Joana shook her head. "I hate to tell you, it ain't working this time. No sir. You know what the sad thing is?"

"What's that?" Tim asked.

Miss Yortsdayle looked on, her smile never wavering as she sipped her tea. Frank was still on the phone pacing in front of the sink.

"What's sad…" Joana continued, "is that I know the exact day that you stopped caring."

"Oh, yeah? And when was that?" Tim leaned into his chair, crossing his arms.

"The first day we had sex. Once I finally put out it was like you finally had what you wanted and had no need to work toward our relationship anymore."

Miss Yortsdayle's eyes went wide. "Getting deep in here… yes… yes it is."

Tim rolled his eyes at his aunt and lifted his mug to his lips, awkwardly avoiding what he would have to say to defend himself.

Joana could tell, he was working through it in his head, trying to come up with words that would somehow, without fail, turn it all around and make it her fault and not his. *Well, if you would have… if you could have… I'm not the one who…* She knew those phrases all too well. She just shook her head. And wasn't having it. Not this time. She had wanted to have this conversation with him for a long time. It had just come down to total chaos and turmoil to force it to the surface. While she sat waiting for him to reply, she realized something. She had been changed. She was so used to getting into it with him and then just giving up as soon as the argument got going. He always won. But now, with all that had happened, her eyes were open. She was her own person. No one, not even the love of her life, was going to stomp all over her feelings and get away with it. If killer koala bears from another dimension weren't going to get away with pushing her around, then why wouldn't that be the case with anybody else?

"She's okay! Thank God! She's made it out!" Frank proclaimed, stuffing the cellphone back into his jeans under his coveralls.

"That's good news. Yes… yes it is. Of course… of course." Miss Yortsdayle nodded from her spot at the table.

"Hell yeah it is," Frank said, his spirit obviously lifted high from hearing the good news.

"So where was she?" Tim asked, turning his attention to Frank, but not before getting glared at by Joana.

"She'd already made it out of town before everything went all orange and shit." Frank smiled, breathing heavy. The weight just seemed to peel away from his shoulders as he leaned against the sink. "She said she's been trying to call me all night. The field-thingy must have been blocking my phone signal. And when your aunt…" he pointed at Miss Yortsdayle, "did that thing with the stone around her neck, my signal must have come back. God, it felt good to hear her voice!"

"I bet…" Tim agreed.

"Like you know what it means to care about someone," Joana snipped under her breath.

Not even paying her any mind, Tim said, "So, did she say what was going down on the other side? You were on the phone for a hot minute."

"Yeah," Frank nodded. "She said the entire town is encased in a huge dome and it's so bright that it's already all over the television. The government has already stepped in, claiming a bunch of nonsense, trying to explain it away. She said that the last she saw on the TV there was a bunch of military and stuff surrounding the dome. They're going to try dropping a bomb on it or something."

"A what?" Joana gasped.

"Don't worry, my child," Miss Yortsdayle assured. "They won't get through. The only way for them to get though is—"

A deafening sonic wave flooded the kitchen cutting the old lady's words short. It was so loud that it wasn't even audible. It was just a wave of pressure that pressed against the face and ears like surge of energy.

Wuv… wuv… wuv… wuvvv…

"What the hell is that?" Frank shouted, almost unable to hear the words come from his own mouth.

"I don't know!" Joana yelled, covering her ears and looking around.

Miss Yortsdayle, not seeming to be affected by the booming sound, rose from her chair and grabbed her cane. She nodded at the others and pointed back toward the front of the house, mouthing the words, *'They're here.'*

As she scooted her way across the kitchen, Tim, Joana, and Frank gathered together. Following the old woman back through the fortune telling room, past the door of slithering beads, and into the storefront living room, they could see them.

All of them.

From the yard just beyond the night sky and the field of orange light there was a mob in mass Joana could only compare to the time she and Tim watched a zombie movie on the late show. The hairy, gray bears were lined for as far as the eye could see. Every last one of them seemed irritated and ready to kill anything that moved. Lifting spears and rocks, they all shouted in one accord, eager to penetrate the field and get to those inside the old rickety house.

Standing at the dusty curtains at the living room window, Joana was about to ask where the wave of noise was coming from. She didn't have to ask. There were three massive elephant-like beasts standing about twenty feet apart just on the other side of the barrier. They were grinding their tusks into the orange field, trying like hell to penetrate it.

"Oh my God… what do we do?"

"Nothing to do," Miss Yortsdayle shouted, looking out the window with the others.

Next to her, Frank leaned up looking out the window, Tim and Joana in front of him.

"What do you mean nothing to do?" Tim shouted over the humming wave of surging sound.

"The portals will go away when they leave," Miss Yortsdayle said, still not needing to cover her ears like the others. "And they will leave when we're all dead. That's how it works. They want to ensure that no one, not even us, can get to their world and wreak havoc like our kind has done so many times before. Nothing we can do."

"But they can't get in here," Joana cried, looking out the window at the more than 300 hundred angry other-worldly creatures. "They'll have to leave sooner or later."

"The backyard!" Tim shouted, then stepped past Frank and ran down the hall toward the kitchen.

Joana followed, leaving Frank and Miss Yortsdayle standing in the storefront looking at the horde of crazed creatures in the road just beyond her yard. The elephants weren't letting up one bit. Grinding their sharp tusks against the field, they tried and tried pressing past it to get in. The bears stood waiting for that moment when they could charge forward, taking the house in one massive swarm of rage.

And then, that was when the sound stopped. The elephants quit grinding at the orange hue of energy. Frank stuck a pinky in each ear and shook his head.

Miss Yortsdayle looked up at him, leaning into her cane with her right hand. With her free hand, she locked eyes with Frank and took him by the arm. "There is one last thing to do, my sweet boy. The stones have one last purpose for tonight to be complete."

"What?" Frank said, leaning closer to her unable to really hear. His ears were still ringing slightly.

"The last part of the plan, my boy. Yes… yes… of course… of course." She chuckled, looking over her shoulder toward the kitchen.

The look in her eyes was one of evil intent and Frank didn't like that one bit. The tension in the air was already growing thick with all of those things in the yard and she was getting all mystical and creepy on him again. He hated it when she did that. Now wasn't the time for her to try training him on the 'Jedi' ways. He needed her to be realistic and help get them out of this mess. Not just make it more confusing. She was good at doing that.

"What?" Frank asked again.

When the little lady moved on him, he didn't even see it coming and honestly couldn't even fathom what the hell was happening. The cane in her hand came apart at the base revealing a sharp shiny blade. Startled, Frank jumped back. But it wasn't him that she lashed out at. She lashed out at herself. The blade slid across her throat like a hand through water. Blood gushed out, splashing Frank all across the front of his overcalls. He gasped, taking her into his arms and falling to his knees, trying to soften her fall.

"What the fuck!" he spat, easing her down.

"Here... ta...ake... this," she gurgled, the blood bubbling from the hole in her neck around the liver spots.

When Frank looked down, she held a stone that he hadn't seen before. It was large and smooth. He took the deep penetrating black stone into his hand. It felt icy cold.

"What am I supposed to... I don't... I don't understand," Frank tried to say.

"You... yo...u don't need to... know, no you don't."

Then the oddest thing happened.

She smiled the most sinister smile that Frank had ever seen; the false teeth in her mouth eerie and cold just like the stone in his hand. She reached up with the last ounce of life she had left and grabbed at the stone in his hand.

Forcing it to stay in his grip, she breathed, "Minoto gindispa she-ba me-to-you."

The stone started to glow and before Frank could determine what was happening, he was looking up at himself. With his back to the floor, his eyes locked with his own, his throat felt hot and wet. He felt cold and tired. The last thing Frank Edelman saw before he died was his arm reaching up, trying to grab at the man that looked like him. His liver spotted, old skin brought it home. But by the time he had it all figured out, it was too late. Frank was dead and Miss Yortsdayle was now enjoying her new, male body. He reached down, yanking the small stone that was on the rope around the old woman's neck. Stuffing it into his coveralls, he smiled.

"They're surrounding the house!" Tim said, stepping back into the storefront living room.

"Oh, my God… What have you done?" Joana screamed!

"It wasn't me. No, no not at all," The new Frank said, letting the old woman's body lay there on the floor as he stood, blood covering his chest and a strange black stone still in his hand.

"What the hell happened?" Tim grimaced, stepping over his aunt's unmoving corpse.

"I just took a... I mean," Frank said. "She just took out a knife and slit her own throat. What was I supposed to do?"

"Why the hell would she do something like that?" Joana cried, covering her mouth with one hand.

"I don't know," Frank said. "See if she's still breathing. I need to go into the kitchen and get some of this blood off of me. Yes... yes... of course."

Before Joana or Tim could say anything, Miss Yortsdayle, who was now in Frank's body, walked through the fortune telling room and into the kitchen.

It was strange hearing with new, young ears. She had been in that old body for so long, she was used to not hearing much. In all of her times of body transfer, this was her first time to take the form of a male. She snickered at that as she reached the door that had the two knobs on it next to the stove. She started to reach down taking the left door handle, but stopped, reaching into her pocket for the phone instead.

She dialed Kathie and waited.

The phone only rang twice before it picked up.

"It's done." Frank paused, listening. "Of course... of course, child. It's me. Don't you trust in me?" Kathie talked on the other end for a moment and then the new Frank said, "Yes.... Yes... I'm going now. Of course, we're going to leave together. Just be there like we planned."

And with that, Frank stuffed the phone away, pulled the necklace from his pocket and tied it around his neck. Stuffing it out of sight, he grabbed the door handle and said a few strange words under his breath. When he opened the door, stepping into what used to be the place she had kept the mugs, he grinned closing the door behind him.

That was the exact moment that Joana realized it.

The field of orange energy. It was fading the darkness of Miss Yortsdayle's yard into itself. The field was taking over again, giving the creatures in the road access to the house.

"Oh shit!" The field is coming back! What do we do? I thought your aunt had it taken care of."

"I thought she did, too!" Tim shuddered, looking through the window at what was happening. He took Joana by the hand and said, "Maybe the stone quit working since she killed herself."

Truth was, the stone was no longer with them in the house, but rather... worlds away, strapped to a new neck, ready to live a new life as planned. You see, the stones have power over even our names. Power over all.

"Is this it?" Joana cried, leaning into Tim.

The creatures crept closer to the house as the field started consuming the yard.

"I guess so." Tim nodded, taking her into his arms. "I... I love you, Joana."

"I love you too, Tim."

That was when she realized what she wished he had realized all night. Rather than filling with panic and fear, watching the yard flood with furry bodies, Joana felt calm, as things seem to slow down around her. As she felt Tim breathing against her, she knew that he felt the same way. She knew... this was the end. Love wasn't something you could just pick up and set down. Moving on when the person you were with didn't meet some unrealistic expectations. Tim was fucked up, this was true. But so was she. And she would be lying if she didn't at least admit that he had to put up with her shit just as much as she did his. Love prevailed. Never wavered. Stayed when the times got tough and the other person's true colors shined through. She leaned up, kissing Tim on the lips. He winced a little, the cut on his lip still fresh, but he kissed her back just the same and just as passionate as the first day they had ever met.

The front door crashed open to a bunch of hissing animal-like grunts.

The funny thing was she was okay with it all.

At least she was going to die with her heart still intact.

The End